WATERLOO STORY

747 7483
954- 741- 7843

0658 03 622   20,
3 45, 18,00
1,
6790012
QUINERITA

WATERLOO STORY

PETER PRINCE

BLOOMSBURY

First published 1998

Copyright © 1998 by Peter Prince

The moral right of the author has been asserted

Bloomsbury Publishing Plc, 38 Soho Square, London W1V 5DF

A CIP catalogue record for this book
is available from the British Library

ISBN 0 7475 3677 5

Typeset by Hewer Text Composition Services, Edinburgh
Printed in England by Clays Ltd, St Ives plc

gentry portilino
ou. VIA - VITTORIA | VIA del conso
via del corso

FOR ROSA

I

1

About a year ago I ran into an acquaintance from my younger, weirder days. The encounter took place at a health club in Putney. I'd been going to it for nearly ten years, since that Christmas break when I realised I had become markedly – though not grossly I should say, in fairness to myself – overweight. In the first year the regime had comprised five full work-outs of ninety minutes each per week, spent among an extensive array of lifting and stretching machines, treadmills, rowing simulators, exer-cycles, etc. In that year I built up by these means an astonishing set of muscles. Unfortunately I also managed in my zeal to very nearly cripple in succession my left arm, my right leg, and finally, most painfully, my back. The frequency and duration of my sessions began to drop away. By now, they were down to one every other week, made up of twenty minutes' gentle toiling on the treadmill. My muscles had all but disappeared from view. On the other hand, my midriff girth, which never seemed to have been much affected when I was exercising all out, also did not appear to increase when I slackened off.

I was bored with the whole carry-on. The health club, and my membership of it, now seemed to belong to another period of my life, like a tired old friendship lingering on

3

well past its allotted time only because, deep in my middle age, I couldn't find the energy to get rid of it. Yet, I had to admit it was still always pleasant after the shower to go down glowing healthily to the restaurant, and sip an orange juice at the bar. The restaurant was one of those light-wood, giant-yucca, vaguely-Mexican-muralled jobs. Various healthies, male and female, all considerably younger than me, sat around at the glass-topped tables that were dotted about the room, chatting and drinking and eating fat-free snacks. I had often assured myself that my purpose in being here was certainly not just to have the opportunity to peep at scantily clad young female bodies. Nothing so sad. On the other hand, in keeping with my now relaxed, not to say self-indulgent attitude towards the club, I could admit to myself that it was one of the perks.

I was watching a very sweet-faced girl at a nearby table. She was wearing a black and mauve lycra outfit that covered her almost from neck to toe. It artfully defined and held taut her body, and I was trying to make out the precise shape and heft of her breasts. Not so easy because she was turned somewhat away from me to talk to her male companion. Who, just as I was craning my head to get a better angle on her, happened to glance up in my direction. I hastily turned away – and found myself staring at another man who had just come up to order at the bar. He was gazing back at me. We nodded politely at each other, as two strangers would, then I looked away again.

I had drained the last of my orange juice, and was wondering whether to order another or else to get out of here, perhaps go in search of a decent movie – it was my half-day off – when the man next to me said:

'I know you, don't I?'

I thought: I hope to God not. Was it a customer I ought

4

to have remembered? A neighbour? One of my ex-wife's friends? I was always running into them, and I never could recall their names. Or faces. I turned, surveyed him more carefully than before. A bulky, fleshy, red-faced fellow in, I estimated, his late forties. Wearing a chalk-striped suit, blue shirt with separate white collar. Club tie. Looked like an estate agent, I thought, of a somewhat superior kind. Commercial property in the West End? Desirable residence is offered in St John's Wood?

And then he smiled at me, and just in that moment I saw something – I remembered somebody, but from very far away. He couldn't then be a customer as I had decided he must be. No, it was a countenance from much earlier than the shop. From ages ago.

'John Brett,' the man said. He held out his hand. 'Hughes & Hughes? . . . I'm John.'

John. John and Lawrence. John and Lawrence and Brian and – I felt suddenly dizzy.

He told me then who I was, and I had to confess it was so. And I remembered it was precisely on that awful day, New Year's Eve '64, that the boys had learned my name for the first time.

'Are you all right?' he said then, leaning towards me, concerned. I must have gone pale, I know I was swaying a bit, and had to find a stool to sit on and steady myself. For just a moment I had been shoved right back into that dusty, draughty, enormous room. And the open window and the ropes dangling, some inside, some out.

'Bit hungry,' I said through clenched teeth. Though the waves of nausea were abiding somewhat. I stared at this bulbous balding fellow next to me. John!

'Have you eaten yet?'

I shook my head.

5

'Fancy a sandwich? I usually have one. Or two. After a work-out.'

John! Of Hughes & Hughes.

'It's good to see you, John,' I said, and I really meant it. *'After all these years . . .'*

2

The Yuletide record that year was 'Blue Christmas'; something of a disappointment this, coming from the King himself and, most fans agreed, not a patch on last year's hit: 'All I Want for Christmas is a Beatle' by Dora Bryan. Of course, the Number One disc was *by* the Beatles: 'I Feel Fine', not a bad addition to the *corpus* but, because I associate it so much with the events I am going to recount, one I have never been able to hear since without experiencing a kind of dread.

What else was going on that winter? The usual for the times, I suppose: wars and massacres, another run on sterling, the Queen pays a state visit to somewhere warm and exotic. Nothing much stands out in my memory. A short while back a Labour government had come to power, and its leader had made a famous promise to forge a new Britain in the 'white heat' of advanced technology. But since I'd been aware of such things, every six months it seemed somebody or other was promising a new era for Britain, and yet nothing much appeared to have changed. Nothing much appeared to have changed this time either. And yet a few short years later one looked back and – lo, everything had changed. The place was unrecognisable. Something must have been going on. Here and there, in ones and twos and tens and scores, and then at last in thousands, in millions, the termites must have been nibbling away at the foundations – otherwise why would the old building have fallen down? If not for the termites.

This isn't my story exactly, and it is enough to state that a couple of years before this time, in my very late teens, I became much afflicted by sadness. I no longer understand the reasons why I put myself and those around me through all that misery. I remember roughly what the reasons appeared to be, but they don't seem now to be at all sufficient. At any rate, one spring day I had tried to kill myself. I believe it was a serious attempt. My room-mate – I was in my first year at university – had set off home for the weekend, and I expected to have forty-eight hours to do what I'd planned. But his car broke down just out of town. He walked back to the flat, found me still breathing, and called the police who called an ambulance. I woke up next morning in hospital, in despair at finding myself alive.

Still I think I took it as a kind of sign, an injunction perhaps, for I never tried doing that again. Subsequently I was treated for depression for a period of three months by a Mr Dysart. Mr Dysart's beliefs depended less on Freud than on his own version of brisk common-sense. He felt that my troubles would be more than half-cured if I could simply learn to stand on my own two feet. 'Regularity of employment,' he told me, 'is a first-class therapist. And a regular pay-packet at the end of each week. Give you a sense of pride. Purpose. Value. Do you see that?'

He spoke of my case to a friend and neighbour of his in Haywards Heath, a Mr Hughes, the managing director of a long-established family firm of hardware merchants, with offices and a warehouse in London. I became an employee. My labours were not onerous, though they were endless. I was provided with a feather duster and asked – asked is the word, it was never Mr Hughes' style to order – to dust each and every item in the firm's stock, a couple of million and more nuts and bolts and clamps and nails and screws. It was a job equivalent to painting the Forth Bridge. Long before I'd finished one complete round of dusting, the first items I had worked on were ready to be dusted again.

'You're not to work too hard, my boy,' Mr Hughes had told me, on the first day, as he showed me around the warehouse. It occupied the top floor of a high Victorian building that stood in the midst of a maze of cobbled streets and alleys on the south bank of the river, a few hundred yards from Tower Bridge, a mile or so east of the Waterloo terminus. 'You're not to strain yourself.' In this way I was introduced to Hughes & Hughes (Est. 1862), and to the warehouse, and to the two stockmen, Brian and Frank, who also worked up there, though very much harder than I did. There was no heat on that floor, except for a small paraffin stove that Frank kept near his desk, and at the far end of the loft was a loading bay, a giant rectangle of a window, floor to ceiling in height, and always open to the sky in working hours. It was freezing cold up in the warehouse, and yet I felt at once at home, and almost happy to be there. And Mr Dysart – whose prescription I was at first inclined to deride – turned out to be right. With regular employment my spirits lifted marginally. From depression I rose to a state of entrenched numbness. I only asked to be left alone, not to have to speak, not even to have my presence acknowledged if that was possible. It puzzled Brian for the first few days. He used to seek me out in whatever dark recess I had taken myself off to, and try to talk to me. But then he got it.

9

'He wants to be invisible,' he told Frank one morning. 'Well, fair enough.'

It was Brian's conviction that anybody's ambitions could be satisfied at Hughes & Hughes, as long as they were modest enough, and as long as they didn't conflict with the nature of the firm, the deep current of its being, a phenomenon that might be characterised as a sort of benevolent near-inertia. He saw that morning that what I wanted in no way threatened that sluggish flow, and that I was certainly modest of aspiration. And so he left me scrupulously alone thereafter. What Kenny wanted, on the other hand, was totally opposed to the historic soul of Hughes & Hughes, and his ambitions, even if he couldn't always clearly articulate them, were tremendous. Violent. So Brian fought him bitterly, in season and out, using all the resources of his authority, his seniority – he'd been with the firm since about 1950 – and, important buzz word of those days, his 'charisma'. Kenny, that acned little mod, nineteen years old, and a year and a half in the job, had none of these qualities and looked to be certainly over-matched in any struggle with Brian. Except I see now that Kenny always had the future on his side.

I lurked in the background, unnoticed, but watching everything. Brian, catching sight of me one day, after a month or more of my 'invisibility', good-humouredly called me 'the Ghost', and I think that was the name I was generally known by throughout the firm. Nobody bothered me much. My lack of response made me an unrewarding target for conversation, flirtation – women outnumbered the men by three to one in that building – or teasing. Even Kenny soon lost interest in trying to wind me up.

'Fuckin' bloke's nuts,' he complained one frosty morning, retreating from the far corner where he'd discovered

10

me ten minutes before. 'Naff cunt. Doesn't say a fuckin' word, and every time you fuckin' talk to him keeps fuckin' movin' away.'

(Kenny was always exceptionally foul-mouthed – very different again from Brian, who I never heard curse except when he was greatly provoked. It used to be very monotonous to hear Kenny speak. It is, I find, just as much so to see it written down. In those days I think the convention still largely held of sanitising filthy words in print. In the name of liberty, it was soon to go. In the interest of reducing tedium when Kenny is on the scene, I plan to return to it.)

'Then leave him alone,' Brian said.

'He's a f—n' lunatic. He's probably dangerous.'

'Go away, Kenny.'

'Make me.'

Brian did. He was a powerful man. Early thirties. Handsome and graceful in his movements, but when he stripped for work on a hot summer day I could see the muscle on him, on his arms and shoulders, working away under the pale skin. In repose, he was like a statue. Physically, Kenny couldn't stand up to him for a second. As soon as Brian took up any of the challenges he threw at him, Kenny – as he did now – would giggle, and slide away, and head for the door. I could hear him then pattering down the stairs.

'Don't come back,' Brian would call after him.

But he always did. Though he had no business to. Like many people, including myself obviously, Kenny had wangled himself into Hughes & Hughes on the back of some hard luck story. Initially he had been assigned to help out in the accounts department on the second floor, but his inability to add up, or take away, or even, it was said, to count past twenty, proved a terminal handicap

11

there. Now he was nominally attached, in various menial capacities, to a number of departments. Nobody could exactly say what his job consisted of, or even who was directly in charge of him, but it was understood at least that his theatre of operations would be confined to the office floors. But as Kenny often said, you can't keep a good man down, and half a dozen times a day at least he would climb the six flights up to the warehouse. He just couldn't stay away. I see why now. Brian was the great enemy, and for that reason was endlessly fascinating to Kenny. But also, I am sure, Kenny admired Brian, would have liked to gain his friendship. I wondered often afterwards if Brian had tried that tactic, had feigned friendship, and got Kenny on his side, whether he'd have come out on top instead. But it's hypothetical. Didn't happen. Anyway Brian was too honest and too . . . primitive is the word, to go in for tricky manoeuvring like that. No, it was the head-down charge for Brian always, come what may.

The other regular inhabitant of the sixth-storey warehouse was Frank. Dear old Frank, in his brown-cloth coat, like a baker's roundsman – there was still such a trade in those days – and his trilby hat. He had – not a speech impediment, not a cleft palate or anything like that, but a way of talking that was all his own, slow and deep and fuzzy, and he ran his vowels together and he skipped his consonants often, so that usually it was nearly impossible to know what he was saying. Though Brian always knew. Frank was forty-odd, thick hands, thick lips. Horn-rimmed National Health spectacles with thick lenses sat upon his broad, thoughtful face. Kenny couldn't stand him.

'My God, with that f—n' Ghost, and this f—n' zombie (pointing at Frank), I reckon you got one and a half brains between you up here.'

Brian caught him a smart crack on the head for that. Above all Brian wouldn't stand for Frank being mocked or insulted. Though Frank himself didn't seem to mind the jeers much, carrying on in his slow way, shuffling the invoices in his solid hands, calling out his lists to Brian in his peculiar voice. Between the two of them they had to make up the orders for shipment to all Hughes & Hughes' customers in the south-east of England. Twice a day, morning and late afternoon, several cratefuls of orders would be winched down from the loading bay to the cobbled street below. Once a day a new shipment of hardware items would arrive by lorry from the suppliers in the Midlands, and be winched up to the warehouse for distribution and storage in the hundreds of tin boxes that lined the tiers of shelves that filled most of the warehouse space. All this was Frank and Brian's job.

And I – I kept to my dim hiding-places, crouched among those many tiers of shelves, and I dusted. Take a handful of nuts, take out a bolt, give them a flick with the duster, put them back. If not the cheapest, our customers certainly got the cleanest nuts and bolts and screws and spanners on the market. It occurs to me that in the time I worked there this was the solitary innovation that Mr Hughes installed to beat back the rising tide of foreign competition. I was it. My feather duster was the 'white heat'. Between us, Kenny and me represented all of the old firm's capacity for innovation, change, the future.

I dusted. And I watched. And I kept out of the way. All the time, without knowing it, I think I was waiting for something to turn up.

3

In a corridor on the ground floor of the old building on Cutt Street, SE, that contained the offices of Hughes & Hughes, two employees of the firm were holding an earnest conversation one morning in December, twelve days before Christmas. A tremendous crash in the street outside interrupted their discussion. Kenny was the first to recover.

'Ignore it,' he said. And again tried to press the Bic ballpoint into the woman's hand.

'But somebody might have been hurt,' the woman said half-hopefully.

She was a lady in her late forties, bottle-blonde, stiletto heels, a tired, good-tempered face, dominated by a pair of vividly painted lips. She was known in the firm (though hardly ever to her face) as 'Hoover'. There was an aura of twenty or twenty-five years ago about her, of fun at the fair, Dreamland, don't mind if I do, one Yank and they're off. Her companion, on the contrary, with his acne and his sneer, his razor-cut hair-do, high-roll collar and tight mod suit, was bang up to date. And much aware of it. Clearly he could hardly bear to spend time with this old relic – though knowing his cause was just, he was prepared to argue with her all day if necessary.

14

'Nobody's been hurt,' he said impatiently. 'Just sign, for Chrissake.'

'Well, I don't know . . .'

Doubtfully the woman bowed her head again over the sheet of paper in her hand. She read what was written on it, her scarlet lips moving slowly as she read. Kenny rolled his eyes up to the low ceiling. The paint on it was cracked and peeling. There were ancient cobwebs in the corners. He studied these signs of decay wrathfully, his sneer growing ever more disdainful as he looked.

At that moment one of the doors along the corridor opened and a man peeped out. A portly man, aged somewhere between fifty-five and sixty; in a decently cut business suit. On his pleasant, ineffectual face, there was an expression of vague concern.

'Did anyone hear a sort of *bang* just now?' he enquired politely.

At the sight of this man, Kenny had snapped into an alert and eager and almost fawning posture.

'Mornin', Mr Hughes,' he cried. 'Lovely morning.'

Mr Hughes gazed at him curiously.

'Kenny Glover,' Kenny said helpfully.

'Of course. Good morning, Kenny. Did you hear –?'

'Morning, Mr Hughes,' the woman simpered.

'Good *morning*, Cynthia. How are you?'

Mr Hughes advanced into the corridor towards her. His voice dropped to a solicitous level.

'Any news of your daughter?'

Behind Mr Hughes' back, Kenny demonstrated his impatience at this new interruption of his great task by making hideous faces and sighing and clicking his teeth loudly.

'She's much calmer now, Mr Hughes.'

'Good. Good.'

'She knows she's been a silly girl. And now she's learning her lesson. And I think she'll be really a different person when it's all over.'

'*Excellent*. And when – how long exactly . . .?'

'She'll be out in another three months.'

Mr Hughes nodded. 'Well, will you tell her, Cynthia, when next you see her, that I'm sure we can find a place for her here when – as soon as she's available.'

'Thank you ever so much, Mr Hughes –'

'Not at all.'

'– but I think she's got other plans.'

For a moment Mr Hughes was taken aback, and he looked a little hurt.

'Well . . . well, just a thought.'

Then, recovering, and after a kindly nod to each of his employees, having evidently clean forgotten what had brought him out into the corridor in the first place, he returned to his office. Kenny swung into action again as soon as the door closed behind him.

'Right. How about it?'

Again the woman shook her head doubtfully.

'I don't want to get into trouble.'

'Hoover! What's the matter with you? This is *nineteen sixty-four*. You got rights.'

'I dunno about that.' She frowned angrily. 'And don't call me that name, you!'

Kenny heaved a final sigh. He shrugged also to show how completely indifferent he was.

'All right. Sign it. Don't sign it. But I'm in a hurry. I promised to take it up to Brian.'

Hoover looked up at that.

'Is Brian going to sign?'

'Brian? He'd be the first to sign –'

'Well, why isn't he?'

'Only he wanted to be the last.'

For a moment she pondered this piece of logic. Then she gave up.

'Oh, heck. If Brian's signing, it must be all right. Give us that pen.'

Without another word, Kenny handed her the Bic. She went over to the wall and, resting the paper against the chipped paintwork, began laboriously to add her name to the list. Kenny watched her eagerly. And then, out of the corner of his eye, seemed for the first time to catch sight of me. His pustulated features screwed up in a snarl. But before he could loose off a stream of invective, Hoover was back at his side.

'There,' she said, handing over the sheet.

Kenny gloated over it. 'You done yourself a favour, Hoover,' he told her, his narrow eyes glistening in triumph.

'Well, I hope so. 'Cause I don't want any trouble.'

Kenny continued to stare at the paper. 'Now I just want one more,' he brooded. 'Just one. All I need.'

'Well, you'll get that from Brian,' Hoover pointed out.

After a moment, Kenny nodded. 'That's right.' He looked up and grinned foxily. 'So you're going to see some big changes round here soon, Hoover. Big changes!'

'I told you,' she flared up again, 'don't call me –'

'Yeah, yeah,' Kenny said boredly, moving away from her. She watched him for a moment, then with a toss of her head, turned and clicked away down the corridor on her murderous heels. Kenny raised his eyes from his paper long enough to call after her:

'Hooo-ver!'

But she didn't look round. Kenny smirked. 'Silly old c—t,' he muttered. He glanced once again at his bit of paper. Then he remembered my presence and looked up again, his thin lips framing threats and oaths. But I was already ahead of him, moving fast towards the stairs.

4

On the top floor the scene appeared much the same as had greeted me on several hundreds of mornings by now. Frank, in his baker's coat, was standing by his 'desk', an old, scarred dining-room table, thick-legged, with drawers at the side. On the table, as always, sat a pile of brown paper bags, and next to them, beside the telephone, the morning's invoices. Frank had his tin open and was happily and seriously engaged in scooping out some of the thick whitish substance it contained, and smearing it on to his palms.

Brian was nearby, sitting on a low trolley, smoking and looking at the back pages of a newspaper. On this day Brian was wearing his black jeans and a creamy-white shirt and a shark-skin grey drape jacket that I always thought looked particularly well on him. The paper he was reading was the *Daily Sketch*, which he bought every morning on his way to work. (I was always a bit puzzled at this choice. From my lunch-break readings of copies thrown away by Brian, I decided it was a pretty feeble paper, and was neither surprised nor cast down when it died at last some time in the early 1970s. But Brian favoured the racing coverage – by 'Gimcrack' – and Jack Hill on the Pools.)

Neither of my colleagues looked up at my entrance, and I kept moving onward to my usual morning refuge. As I rounded the first tiers of shelves I saw that, in fact, something was very different about the sixth floor today. Standing back there, just in sight of the desk, I found two boys of about seventeen, fresh-faced, both wearing blue jeans and woolly jumpers. They looked rather scared, and as if they were waiting for something to happen. I didn't know who they were, though I thought as I went by that there was a flicker of recognition in the eyes of the taller one. I don't think the other even noticed me. I settled down in my place, between two tiers, and wondered who these boys were. And whether they were here to stay. I hoped not, desiring – as I believed I did – that nothing in the warehouse should ever change.

Brian threw his cigarette away at last and got up and went to the phone. He dialled '9' for the outside line, and then seven numbers.

'Mickey? Yeah, Brian. All right.' He glanced down at the newspaper. 'I'll have No Reply in the two-thirty and, ah, Prince of Erin in the three o'clock. Three quid each way . . . Right. Cheers.'

He hung up. Then turned and surveyed the two boys. There was, I could see, a particularly grim expression on his handsome face as he walked towards them.

'Now then, you two.'

The boys came to a sort of attention. Brian looked at the taller boy.

'You were here last year.'

'Yes,' the boy breathed.

'We had to do it all over again after you'd gone, did you know that?'

The taller boy shook his head unhappily. I remembered him now. He'd worked here last Christmas, doing the

20

inventory. He'd got the job because his father was a friend of Mr Hughes. I don't think we ever said a single word to each other, and so his stay hadn't been a problem for me at all. I breathed easier, remembering that.

Brian took out a packet of Senior Service cigarettes, lit one up. He studied the taller boy all the time.

'You're –?'

'John.'

The other boy spoke up quickly.

'I'm Lawrence.'

Brian ignored him.

'Remember how to do it, John?'

'Well . . .'

'Give 'em pencils, Frank.'

Solemnly, carefully, Frank opened a drawer in his desk. If you didn't know him, and love him – as I did – there was always something comical about the way Frank moved. I could see the boys found it comical. The one called John nudged the other, and both tittered surreptitiously. Brian was watching them closely. Finally Frank came up with a couple of stubby pencils and handed them to the boys. They were still – especially the smaller kid, Lawrence – killing themselves with silent, nervous laughter.

'All right – ' Brian pointed at Lawrence. 'Pick out that end box.'

Lawrence stooped and drew out a box from one of the lower shelves. It contained eight-inch reaper files, I knew. I tried to remember if I'd dusted that row recently. (I had a pretty good system, but sometimes it broke down, meaning usually that I found myself dusting items twice over.) I hoped I had. I wanted these boys to know we had standards up here. Even if we seemed like clowns to them.

'What does it say on the bit of paper?'

21

Lawrence screwed up his eyes to read the pencilled words on the paper strip that was gummed to one end of the box. Frank's writing was never easy to decipher.

'"Eight-inch reapers",' he said at last.

'And there's a number.'

'"Sixty-eight".'

'Count 'em,' ordered Brian.

The boy started on the task, slowly and inexpertly. Brian watched impatiently for a while, then glanced at the other boy.

'You still at school, John?'

The boy nodded.

'Workin' hard?'

'Well, you know . . .' The boy shrugged. 'Yeah. S'pose so.'

'That's right,' Brian nodded approvingly.

Lawrence finished his task.

'Thirty-four,' he announced.

'Right. You cross out the sixty-eight. Write in the thirty-four . . . Go on. Do it.'

Lawrence did it.

'Now you need a sheet of paper . . .' Brian crossed swiftly to the desk. 'Couple bits of paper, Frank.'

Methodically, Frank opened his drawer again, and took out a pad of exercise paper. Brian stood beside him, waiting as Frank's thick hands manoeuvred for a grip on the paper. Not a trace of impatience showed on Brian's face, but softly he pounded the top of the table with one fist as Frank, with an expression of great concentration, began to tear the first sheet off.

I saw John give the other boy a nudging grin as they watched him. But his companion didn't smile. He looked quite scared.

Brian at last came back to them gripping the sheets of paper. He gave one to each.

'All right,' he told Lawrence. 'You write down at the top "eight-inch reapers".' He kicked the tin. 'How many?'

Lawrence stooped to read his own writing. Brian, waiting, snapped his fingers.

'Thirty-four.'

'Put it down on the paper. That's what you do. Count 'em up. Change the number on the box. Write it down on the paper. That's the job.' He glanced at John. 'Remember now?'

The boy nodded. Brian grabbed his arm and led him over to another tier of shelves.

'You start here. I don't want you talking.'

Brian waited for a while until the boys, at their separate stations, were settled in. Then he went back to the desk. I saw John look up from his work and over at Lawrence. But the other boy kept his head down, kept counting steadily.

'Let's do 'em, Frank,' Brian said. He picked up the slim pile of invoices, and weighed them in one hand. 'What there is of 'em,' he added moodily. He took off his drape jacket then and hung it on a wire hanger. From the hanger he took a crimson bandana and tied it around his black, sculpted hair. Then, pausing to grab half a dozen brown paper bags from the desk, he went and positioned himself in the middle of the gangway, halfway down the warehouse. He flexed his arms, flexed his legs, then looked back at Frank.

'Ready!' he called.

Ponderously, Frank sorted through the invoices. Then he laid the pile back on the desk and picked the top one off and studied it through his thick lenses.

'"Seven-eighth nickel screws, fifty-six",' Frank read out at last.

23

5

To me by now the morning and afternoon calling-out of the orders was like a litany, familiar and predictable, part of the unchanging life of the warehouse, of Hughes & Hughes, that I loved so much. I had long ago stopped thinking that there was anything strange about this ritual, specifically about the sounds that came out of Frank's mouth during his part in it. But of course there was. Something very strange. Frank's thick tongue twisted and liquefied the words so that the order he had just called came forth sounding something like 'Sen-eigh' nicke' 'rew fif'ix.' Add to that the deep booming fuzzy tone of his voice, which hit the ear very like a foghorn on a foggy night. Add in, I suppose, the tension of anyone starting a job, the first day, even a Christmas job. Add also the fact that the boys were young and being so couldn't help being a bit callous . . . Suffice to say, Frank's first utterance immediately tipped both boys off into wild hysteria. I could see their shoulders shaking as they tried to control themselves. Lawrence was holding his hand over his mouth to stifle his giggles. John was not quick enough, and a single scream of laughter escaped him before he could choke it back.

I didn't know, didn't look to see if Frank had noticed.

After a moment or two of checking the boys' reaction, I turned quickly to look at Brian. I would never willingly miss this part of the daily ritual. As soon as Frank had finished speaking, Brian made a leap upwards and sideways and grabbed on to a tier of shelves. Two quick hand-over-hand movements brought him to the top shelf on the tier. There he drew out a tin box. Grabbed a handful of screws and dropped them one after the other, very fast, into a paper bag. Then another handful. Then another, a bit smaller. Then he looked down at Frank.

'Yeah?'

'"Four-inch Cromptons, two dozen',' Frank bellowed forth. ('Fo' in' Cromp'ans to'uzzin'.)

On the instant, Brian leaped from the tier he was on to its neighbour. Then jumped, soared through the air, clung on to another tier. He dropped down this tier to the second shelf above the floor. He reached in and pulled out a tin.

'Haven't got 'em. Next?'

'"'ree-in' 'oach 'crews, 'ree and a ha' 'ozen".'

Up the side of the tier, just like a cat. Then in two bounds – one across the gangway, then over the spot where I was crouching – Brian fetched up on the tier at the bottom of which Lawrence knelt, giggling unhappily. He began counting out the three-inch coach screws. I waited patiently for his next move. I never got tired of watching Brian fill the orders. His leaps and his jumps – later in life I became for a time very interested in classical ballet, almost an aficionado. But at this period I had not yet even seen my first performance. And yet I sensed – and I was correct in this – that the feeling I got watching Brian at work must be akin to what ballet enthusiasts saw in the art. That grace and harmony of motion, those figures cut against the sky . . . Yet there was something

25

tougher and more dynamic in Brian's performance than I – somewhat erroneously, I was to discover – imagined that ballet could ever offer. There was a robustness, like a great acrobat, or a Spanish dancer – or bull-fighter . . . power, virility, all without a trace of pretension on the part of the performer. And all this was mine to watch, twice daily in that warehouse. I close my eyes now, I can still see him bounding through the dusty air, from tier to tier. I think of animals, great cats, panthers . . . and then I see him waiting for his next direction, alert, tensed, his fabulous capability held in check by the slow, near-incomprehensible man in the brown coat standing at the desk. Beauty in the thrall of the Beast.

(Needless to say, I did not share these wild thoughts with my colleagues on any of the floors of Hughes & Hughes. The fact that I never talked with anyone served to protect them as much as me.)

So Brian, having signalled that he had completed filling the item, waited, clinging to his tier, for Frank to send him on his way again. The seconds ticked by, Frank peered at the invoice in his hand. I heard Brian give out a low long moan of frustration.

Frank at last set the paper down on the table.

'That's all,' he said. (''as' orl.')

No doubt rendered extra tense by Brian's position on a shelf above him, young Lawrence let out a splutter of nervous laughter. Brian landed softly on the floor beside him.

'Having a little chuckle at Frank, are we?'

Lawrence looked up, very scared, at the powerful man beside him. I noticed that John, at his shelf, was keeping his head well down, and counting screws furiously. Brian looked Lawrence over carefully. Then, still very quietly:

'Did you know he was tortured by the Japs?'

26

Lawrence shook his head numbly.

'For twenty days and twenty nights.'

The boy looked on the brink of tears.

'On the last night,' Brian sighed, 'they cut his cock off. Did you know that?'

The boy couldn't look away. His mouth hung open. Brian nodded slowly.

'You'd better come and have a look.' He grabbed Lawrence by the arm and began to pull him towards the desk. 'Er, Frank,' he called out. 'Moment of your time.'

The boy managed to wrestle himself away.

'No! I don't want to look!'

Brian stared at him for a moment. And then he chuckled. Lawrence stumbled back to his shelf. I doubted the boy would believe the 'tortured by the Japs' story for long after he got his wits back. I also guessed it would be a very long time – if ever – before he was tempted to snigger at Frank again. Brian followed him, and stood over him as, still very shaken, he started back on his counting. At that moment, from where I was crouching, I could see that Kenny had appeared in the doorway.

6

It was Kenny's almost invariable custom, when he visited the warehouse for the first time on a particular day, to creep in on tip-toe and then, when he was just behind Frank, to roar out a greeting at the top of his voice. The reaction this created in poor Frank was always cheering to Kenny. This time, however, I saw that Kenny was coming in quite openly, walking with regular footsteps, wearing a smile that, at a guess, was intended to be ingratiating.

'Good mornin', Frank,' said Kenny heartily, but at no exaggerated volume. 'How are you doing?'

Frank, who for many good reasons loathed Kenny, glanced around and grunted in a highly unwelcoming manner. Kenny's smile didn't waver. He reached into the inside pocket of his tight-fitting jacket, and brought out a sheet of paper. I recognised it as the one he had given Hoover to sign.

'Now, Frank,' said Kenny earnestly, 'do you remember that little chat we were having the other –'

At that moment Brian stepped down into the gangway, placing himself directly in Kenny's line of vision. Like lightning, the sheet of paper disappeared back into Kenny's pocket, and he smiled weakly.

'Oh, hello, Brian.'

'What do you want?'

Kenny improvised on the spot.

'Just come up to see – uh – see if you wanted anything, Bri.'

A second or two, then Brian nodded. 'Yeah. I do. Cup of tea and a buttered roll. Frank?'

There was an assenting grunt from the desk. Brian turned towards the shelves.

'Boys?'

The two boys came nervously into the gangway. Kenny's eyebrows rose in surprise.

'What are they doin' here?'

After a moment, Brian deigned to reply.

'Invent'ry. Till New Year's.'

The boy called John smiled timidly.

'Hello, Kenny.'

'I remember you,' Kenny said darkly. 'You was here last year. They had to do it all over again when you left.'

John hung his head.

'What do they need two of you for?' Kenny looked at Brian, again an ingratiating leer passed over his narrow face. 'F—k it up twice as bad.'

Brian didn't bother to respond. Disappointed, Kenny turned back to the boys. He looked them over with disapproval.

'They ain't got any stuff on,' he said. He turned suddenly and raced across to the desk. 'Frank. Frank. Here! Give us your tin.'

He rummaged wildly among the papers on the desk, spilling them everywhere. Frank beat out at him ineffectually. 'Go away,' he cried out. 'Go away!'

'Go'ay!' Kenny howled in scornful imitation. 'Go'ay!'

He found Frank's tin. Tossed it up in the air and caught it. Then ran a few steps and bowled it down the gangway

29

towards the boys. Lawrence caught it. He stood staring at the white gunge inside.

Brian looked up. 'It'll help you when you wash your hands,' he advised.

Lawrence took up a small smear of the stuff on his forefinger. He looked down at the white dribble somewhat shrinkingly.

'It's Frank's come!' Kenny chortled.

From the boys a shuddering silence. Brian couldn't help laughing – and was immediately angry with himself for it.

'Get out, Kenny,' he rapped. 'Go and get the tea.'

'I ain't getting these f——n' boys no f——n' tea.'

Brian stared at him. Kenny shook his head.

'I ain't,' he said again. Then he looked towards the desk, raised his voice: 'You listenin' to this, Frank? It's all what I been telling you. Where's it written down anywhere I got to get tea for these two little public-school tossers? So it's a f——n' liberty. That's all it is. And I ain't doing it. No way. I got rights!'

Frank paid no attention to this speech. The boys, I could see, were embarrassed at the fuss they had inadvertently caused. Brian sighed.

'You'd better do it, Kenny.'

'Make me.'

Events then followed their predictable course. Brian surveyed his skinny antagonist wearily. Kenny balanced himself on the balls of his feet and raised his fists. After a moment, Brian took a couple of steps towards him. Immediately, Kenny giggled and dropped his fists and turned away towards the door. Brian looked back at the boys.

'Sugar?'

'Two, please,' John said.

'None for me,' said Lawrence.

'And, Kenny –' Brian called. Kenny looked back. 'I'm planning on a quiet day. You look out for Hughes down there.'

'All right,' Kenny grunted.

'You got that?'

'I said so.'

At the door, Kenny looked round once again.

'Here – who bunged that crate out of the bay this morning?'

Brian and Frank said nothing. I saw the boys were looking sheepish, especially John. After a moment he said: 'Well, I was showing Lawrence . . .' He stopped. Glanced round at the loading bay at the far end of the room. It was festooned with the ordered tangle of pulleys and ropes used for winching crates down and up. John hesitated, was unable to avoid the pun. 'Was showing him the ropes.'

Kenny shook his head. He looked concerned, responsible, censorious. It was strange to see that expression on him, so wild and irresponsible. I wondered if I was seeing the face of Kenny fifteen or twenty years hence.

'You could have killed somebody, you know. If they was standin' underneath . . . Isn't that right, Bri?'

Brian ignored him. Kenny looked back at John. The righteous look slipped from his face like a toy mask. He giggled.

'Be a laugh though if anybody *was* underneath. Strawberry jam! Eh, boys?'

'Kenny.'

'Yes, Bri?'

'I'm waiting for my tea.'

'C—t,' snarled Kenny as he went out of the warehouse, but not very loud.

31

7

When he had finally gone, Brian turned to the boys. He took the tin out of Lawrence's still somewhat nerveless fingers. 'Here,' he said, quite kindly, and got a good dab of the goo from the tin and slapped it into Lawrence's outstretched palm. 'Rub it well in.' He handed the tin to John then. 'You do the same.' He watched the boys rubbing the stuff into their hands, then glanced across to the desk. Frank had got a Mars bar out of his coat pocket and was slowly unpeeling the wrapper. Brian watched him for a moment, then looked back at the boys.

'What did you do with your money from last year, John?' he asked.

'Bought a guitar,' John said shyly.

'Yeah? Can you play it?'

John shrugged modestly. Brian looked at Lawrence.

'Is he any good?'

Lawrence nodded.

'He plays too,' John said. 'We're in the same group.'

Brian studied the boys.

'I'd like to hear that. D'you play anywhere?'

'Pubs. Youth clubs . . .'

'One pub,' Lawrence chipped in wryly. 'One youth club.'

'Want a job on a liner?'

The boys gaped at Brian. John was the first to recover.

'What liner?'

'Something I'm thinking of doing,' Brian said casually. He stooped over and beat out with his palms an intricate rhythm on his thigh. 'I been working on the old brushes lately. Reckon I could get on a boat, cruise ship, play in the band.'

(This was the first I'd heard of it, that Brian was thinking of leaving. I couldn't tell whether he was serious or not. He sounded serious. I crept closer to the gangway so as not to miss a word. The idea that he might go filled me with dread.)

'Yeah,' Brian nodded, resting his palms at last. 'There's jobs on those boats. P & O. White Star. South Africa. Caribbean. Very nice . . . 'Course if you could offer 'em a bit more: drums, say, couple of guitars, singer – a *combo* . . . really make some money then. What do you think, boys?'

The boys were too amazed to speak. Brian looked them over.

'Whyn't you go and get your guitars? We'll see what you sound like.' He looked at John. 'Where do you live?'

'Barnes,' John said breathlessly.

Brian thought it over, turned to the other boy.

'You live near him?'

Too excited to speak, Lawrence nodded.

'And you can both play a bit? No kidding?'

Both together nodded eagerly. But then Lawrence frowned.

'Only it's no use,' he sighed. 'We couldn't take jobs. We're still at school.'

'Well,' said Brian after a moment, 'that's true. That's the important thing. You got to finish school.'

'I don't,' John said. 'I'd leave that dump any time. If there was something good to go to.' He looked hard at his friend. 'And that's what you've been saying too.'

The boys exchanged stares. Lawrence nodded then. 'Yes. That's true.' He looked at Brian. He took a deep breath. 'Yes, I'd leave. I would.'

'Sure?' asked Brian.

'*Sure*,' said the boys together.

'Right,' said Brian.

I watched him as he walked down the gangway to where his drape jacket hung. He had to reach past Frank to get it. Frank had finally swallowed the last identifiable morsel of Mars bar that was in his hand, and was now, with infinite care, searching the front of his coat for any chocolate flakes that might have escaped his mouth. From his jacket, Brian took out a black leather wallet, the size of a paperback book. He came back to the boys. He held out to them a pound note.

'Take a taxi,' he said.

John took the banknote, but neither boy moved from the spot. They looked at each other, then back at Brian.

'But what if Mr –?'

'Don't worry about *him*. I'll take care of Hughes. Be back in an hour, eh?'

At that the boys sprang to life. They hurried over to the pegs near the desk, to retrieve their raincoats. They stood there buttoning themselves up. I saw them glancing over their shoulders, wondering if Brian would change his mind. But he only nodded at them, encouragingly.

When they were gone, Brian stood motionless for a moment in the centre of the gangway. Then he walked slowly back to where his jacket hung, so as to stuff his wallet away.

'How about a liner for the rest of the winter, Frank?' he asked. 'Cape Town . . . Mediterranean . . .'

Frank was engaged in trying to take a tiny speck of chocolate off the sleeve of his coat. He was pursuing it over the cloth with the concentration of a hunter of big game, the dark speck jumping nimbly away each time from his thick, following fingers. He realised at last that he'd been spoken to, and looked up with an expression of bewilderment.

'Wha'?' he said.

Brian, standing behind him, watched him for a moment. Then he smiled and laid his hand gently on Frank's back.

'Nothin',' he said.

He picked up another brown paper bag from the desk, and wandered back to the middle of the gangway. He stood there, staring at the floor-planks. He seemed, as I watched him, to look suddenly tired, as if something vital was ebbing away from him, like blood, or hope.

'Bit of fun on a cold day,' he sighed at last.

Then, like a dog in water, he seemed to shake himself. I saw his energy return. His body seemed to swell, become firm again. He brought the paper bag up to his lips and blew it open.

'Come on, Frank. Let's get on with it.'

And I found myself breathing much easier. I could see I was not going to lose Brian after all. Bit of fun on a cold day. 'If you were dictator of the whole world, what would you do?' It was that kind of thing. It got you through a dull morning. Brian had been carried away for a little while; warmed up by the presence of the boys, the chance to secure their admiration. He had been indulging in a

35

little harmless showing-off. Nobody would be the loser by it, except it had cost Brian a pound to dream for a few minutes.

And except – I thought of the boys now, hurrying west in a taxi, looking forward to their new lives . . . Caribbean . . . Mediterranean . . . well, it would be a bit of a disappointment for them, but – but they were only temporaries after all, not really part of our world. Expendable certainly, if they gave Brian a few good minutes.

8

Frank was rubbing his spectacle lenses between thumb and forefinger to clear the glass. He replaced them carefully on his nose. He picked up the next invoice on the pile. I settled back in a position where I would have a good sight of the action.

'"Two-inch Brads, three dozen",' Frank called out – rather his version of it.

As if to demonstrate what forces dreaming can unlock, the leap that Brian made then was the finest of the whole morning, whole week actually. I could hardly stop myself applauding. From a standing start, he was up on the sixth rung of a tier in one bound, and then, not pausing at all to steady himself, had swept on across the gangway to the tier next to it. There he began filling his paper bag at unprecedented speed.

'Yeah?'

'"Two-inch masonry, five dozen".'

Brian jumped off that tier with a force that left it shuddering, landed catlike on the floor, ran – one step, two, three – then blasted off in a lunge at the top rung of a tier across the gangway. He plunged his hand into a box, came up with a fistful of masonry nails.

I was so wrapped up in the performance that Kenny's

37

reappearance was almost as much of a shock to me as to Frank.

'ALL RIGHT, FRANK?' came the roar from over by the door.

I looked across to see poor Frank – in a clumsy reproduction of Brian's art – hopping a full foot in the air. Kenny was grinning, fit to split his narrow face. In his hands was a tray on which were four mugs and a heap of rolls. He easily dodged the angry swipe that Frank aimed at him.

'Here we go, gents,' he said, as he placed the rolls and a mug of tea each for Brian and Frank on the table-top. 'Nice and hot.'

Holding the tray with the other two mugs on it, Kenny continued along the gangway, looking for the boys. He was outraged when he found they were gone.

'I don't believe it. I f——n' don't believe it.'

'Go away, Kenny,' Brian said from his high perch. He was watching Frank who was taking his time recovering from the shock Kenny had given him.

'I walk up and down those f——n' stairs – out of the kindness of my heart – and those little c—s don't even have the f——n' courtesy –'

'Here, Kenny,' Brian called.

Kenny looked up. Directly above him, Brian was holding out a heavy G-clamp.

'Catch.'

Brian opened his fingers. The G-clamp dropped. Kenny let out a yelp of fear and, to catch the clamp before it hit him, let go of the tray. Hot tea cascaded down his legs, soaking through his smart, flimsy trousers. He writhed in agony, he shouted his anger at Brian, the oaths pouring out of his contorted lips, all one long curse.

I heard Frank roaring with honest laughter over by the

desk. I was watching Brian. He was staring down at Kenny in his pain, and I saw dislike, contempt in his eyes. Most of it for Kenny I am sure – but I couldn't help suspecting that just a little of it might be directed at himself. As if he was rather ashamed of what he'd just done. This was not a good feeling for me. By now, anything Brian did was all right in my eyes, I respected him so much. If, for instance – to take the present example – he felt that in the course of events somebody had earned a scalding, then I'd go along with that. Believing in Brian, I did not have to trouble myself with sorting out any such issues on a personal basis. And too as long as I was sure that he believed in himself utterly, then I knew we were safe and nothing would change; month in and month out, for years ahead, we would be all right, up there on the sixth floor, Brian and Frank and – invisibly – me. But if Brian should start to doubt himself, well . . . well, I didn't know. But I thought we might be heading for trouble.

9

During our lunch break, the boys returned. Frank was eating egg sandwiches and their cloacal aroma lay heavy all around his desk. Brian, consequently, had wheeled the loading-trolley, which was his favourite seat, some way off, and was reclining on it, smoking, drinking tea, and reading a crumpled James Bond paperback. He didn't look up when the boys came in. They were carrying guitar cases, and both looked excited. I could see they were taken aback by how little of a stir their reappearance had caused.

'With you in a minute, boys,' Brian murmured, his eyes tracing the lines on the page.

He turned to the next one. The boys looked at each other, then visibly put their disappointment aside. They propped their guitars against the side of the desk, and took off their raincoats. They removed their instruments, then crossed over to a pile of sacks that lay between two tiers, where in fact I was sitting, biting on an apple. I got up before they arrived, and gave them possession. They sat down on the sacks, and took their guitars reverently out of the cases.

'Give us a G,' John said.

Lawrence struck a chord.

'No, a G.'

I saw Brian lift his eyes from his book and glance over towards the sacks as the tuning-up sounds drifted over to him. Then he turned another page and went on reading. I was beginning to wonder if his apparent reluctance to hear what the boys could do was a tactic to diminish their hopes before they got started. After all, he had been promising them cruise liners before they went away – and though it was all clearly impossible, anyone could see that, still he would have some explaining to do if they were any good.

In the end, after about five more minutes of discordant tuning, Brian got up, parked his book on a shelf, and went over to the sacks. He pulled an empty wooden crate towards him and sat down opposite the boys. He pattered a little with his hands against the side of the crate, then looked up expectantly.

'Right. What have you got?'

If he had been having any worries about how he was going to let them down over the promised Caribbean tour, the boys made it very easy for him. They were atrocious. Let me try to describe how bad they were in this way: before I fell ill, long before I became the Ghost, I was an apparently fairly normal youth, with the interests of a teenager of my day. A few years older than the boys, I had been of the first generation in England to be afflicted with the post-war guitar craze – or plague, as I came to see it. I was a member of a skiffle group, in fact, and as such, with my guitar and my weedy voice, helped three other youths – washboard, tea chest bass, banjo – to murder quite a few fine old negro spirituals, shouts, and work-songs. I can say nothing worse about John and Lawrence's performance than that on this showing they would not have been allowed into my skiffle group.

They began by looking at each other with anxious

grins. Then John started strumming an uncertain chord. Lawrence joined in after a few bars, and it was immediately apparent that, with all the time they'd been given, they still hadn't managed to tune their instruments together. A slight frown appeared on Brian's brow, but he beat his hands on the crate in an attempt to give them a percussion backing. This was not easy as they were playing at different tempos. A couple of false starts – and then the boys broke into song.

It was 'The Times They Are A-Changing'. I know that because a day or two later I heard the boys arguing over who had got the words most wrong, and this was the title they gave it. It was not a song I'd heard before, though of course it was to become wearyingly familiar in later years, as it turned into one of those 'anthems of a generation', of which there seemed to be so many in the 1960s. That decade had only just begun in a real sense, and then not everywhere, and one of the places it certainly hadn't yet reached was our warehouse. Poor John and Lawrence were bringing us the latest thing, if we had but known it. And when I came to think about it long afterwards it was of course an almost too-perfectly appropriate song to sing in present company. But all I at least heard at the time was an awful, lugubrious, tuneless noise. And looking away from the boys, it was clear that I was not alone in hearing this. The frown on Brian's forehead had deepened considerably after the first verse. After the second, he had given up. He stopped beating on the crate. He sat back and glared at the boys as they struggled on. By now they were so far out of synch with each other, they could have been singing a round-song. I glanced over towards the desk. Frank had his head down and was grimly trying to remove the wrapper off a Crunchy bar. I thought I saw him wince once when

John, who had far the louder voice, tried to claw his way to victory at the last by imitating the lonesome sound of a distant freight train. Lawrence did his best to sing on in the face of this constant hooting, but he was obviously not pleased, and cries of 'What are you doing?' and 'Shut up, John!' mingled strangely with what I could understand of the ominous keening of the verse.

It came at last to a ragged, indefinite end. To be followed by a resounding silence. Brian stood up. And if I had thought before that he had been looking for a way to get out of his cruise-liner promises, now I almost believed that there had been a grain of hope in him, just a dream that if he had found a pair of likely young musicians to team up with, then this fantasy could have been made real. By drum and guitar across the Seven Seas. With one bound, Brian frees himself from Hughes & Hughes and joins the world of romance, adventure, foreign parts, James Bond. Yes, I think it must have shimmered mirage-like before him that the boys would have the stuff of genius in them, or at least of competence. For it certainly made him very bitter to find out that they hadn't.

'That was terrible.'

The boys at first were too startled to be crushed by the verdict. They stared up at Brian.

'That was so *bad*.'

He turned away angrily from them.

'Go on. Get back to work.'

He walked away. The boys sat there for a time, slumped over their guitars, their failure soaking into them like toxic rain. Then, not looking at each other, they opened their cases and started to put the instruments away. I looked over to where Brian stood, near the desk, his back to me, seeming to be staring at Frank. Frank was keeping his head down, either because he was so busy with his sweet, or from not wanting to get involved in his colleague's fury. I looked back at the boys. John had closed his case and was fastening the locks, Lawrence's case was still open. He'd stopped trying to shut it. He just sat there, and he looked completely miserable. I felt bad for them both, and wished I could help.

'What do you want to waste time on stuff like that for?'

Brian had returned. He was glaring down at the boys. I felt he was over-reacting. The boys had been bad, had been very bad, but still they had tried hard for him. I was glad to see that John, at least, was beginning to want to fight back.

'It's a good song.'

'It's rubbish.'

'And we know other songs.'

'What songs?' Brian demanded.

There was a pause, and then Lawrence ventured: '"Blowing in the Wind".'

'"Blowing in the Wind",' Brian snorted with huge derision. 'Go on. Work!'

He started back towards the desk. Maybe it was the sight of Frank – whose way of eating Crunchies was to suck the middle out while leaving the chocolate standing – that caused him to turn back almost at once to the boys again. He contemplated them, still wrathfully, but not as much now as if they had handed him a savage personal insult.

'I'll sing you a *song*,' he said at last.

The boys looked up and I could see they were quite interested. Lawrence still hadn't closed the lid on his case. Brian pointed to him.

'Come on. It's just three chords.'

Willingly, Lawrence got his instrument out, and tucked

44

it under his arm. He looked up expectantly. Brian balanced himself, legs spread, hands wavering slightly. Just to see him prepare was impressive. At length, feeling himself ready, he nodded at Lawrence.

'All right . . . C.'

Lawrence launched into a cantering strum. I thought his playing was much more controlled than before, and could see he was trying hard for Brian. But Brian wasn't pleased.

'Slower.'

Lawrence dropped from a canter to a trot.

'Slow-er!'

Lawrence slowed down to a funeral pace. Satisfied at last, Brian shut his eyes, held up his right arm, opened his mouth . . .

> 'I'll be ho-o-ome' ('F!')
> 'My-iy da-a-arlin'' ('C!')
> 'Please wa-a-ait for me.
> I'll walk you home in the
> Moo-oo-oonlight,
> Once more our love will be free.'

After Brian had got fully involved in the song, and no longer remembered to call out the chord changes, Lawrence soon lost his way. Still he plugged on and at least kept some sort of noise going beneath the much greater noise that Brian was sending forth. He had a huge, powerful, mostly flat-sounding voice. I had heard him before over the years, humming and singing around the warehouse, but never at this volume. And I had never watched him *deliver* a song before, and that turned out to be a sight to see. I remembered this number, as it happened. At least I remembered a neutered version

45

of it, released by Pat Boone a few years before. Save for the American accent which both singers employed, Brian's interpretation was very different. For as he sang he clawed the air, and rolled his eyes, and shook his head wildly from side to side. He'd bend his knees almost to the ground, and then jump high in the air – not at all in the balletic manner in which he filled the daily orders, but like the spasms of a wild beast, captive and lunging at its tormentors from the end of its tether. He staggered often, and sometimes he almost fell to the ground; once he did just that, and yet never missed a word or a note during the accident, just kept on bellowing tragically as he leaped back on to his feet, en route to further, greater exertions. I never saw its like again, until some five years later when I was no longer the Ghost, and I went to a Joe Cocker concert (is Joe Cocker still remembered/ever heard of?). And what I saw on *that* evening looked to me like a restrained version of Brian's performance on the sixth floor that afternoon.

The boys were thunderstruck. Frank stopped eating sweets. I didn't know how to feel. It was very funny. In another way it was like watching a soul in torment.

'So dar-lin' –' (Brian sobbed. 'F!')
'As I write this le-e-tter,
Here's hoping' – (No!)

Lawrence gave up. Brian hurtled on, all alone.

'You're thinkin' of me-e-e.
My mind's made up
So long un-til
I'll be home to start se-e-ervin' yo-o-ou . . .'

46

He flapped his arms wildly and bent his head back as far as it would go and we knew he had reached the climax of his song. We all leaned forward breathlessly. I was willing him to hit that note, the others were too I was sure.

'I – I – I'll bee-e-e –'

Ah, but he couldn't do it. Not quite. That last note, that final 'home' that should have rung out like a bugle call, skidded into a breathy falsetto. And then Brian was seized by a racking fit of coughing. He waved his arms about in frustration and with the effort of getting his breath back. The boys clapped frantically. Even I felt like doing something to show my appreciation, at least for the effort Brian had put into it.

A bland and cheerful voice broke into our diversions.

'Jolly good, Brian! Unexpected talents.'

We all swung round to look towards the door. Mr Hughes was standing there, beaming. Evidently he'd been there for some time. John and Lawrence got awkwardly to their feet. I looked at Brian. He had flushed a deep crimson.

Mr Hughes strolled a little way into the warehouse.

'And how are the boys doing? Working hard, are they?'

Brian wouldn't even look at his boss. It was left to Frank to mumble something that could have been 'All right'.

'Good. Excellent,' smiled Mr Hughes. 'And now . . .' He glanced down at the watch on his wrist. 'If the concert's over . . . they're crying out for the orders downstairs.'

He was clearly so delighted to have caught Brian out. It was understandable, for – poor man – even his own secretary used to say that Hughes & Hughes was run

47

more to suit the chap on the sixth floor than anything else. And by that she certainly wasn't referring to Frank, or to me. Though the kindest of men, Mr Hughes had his pride, and revenge was sweet for him that afternoon. I saw him shoot a quick glance at Brian, and I was sure he was wondering whether he could press his advantage any further. But wisely he decided to settle for what he had. He bestowed on us all a last paternal beam, and then turned and walked out. We could hear him humming as he went down the stairs.

10

My eyes went back to Brian. His face was terrible to see.
I looked at Frank who had got up while Mr Hughes was
in the room. He was still standing, and looking at Brian
with what appeared to me like great concern. He cleared
his throat uneasily. The boys too were watching Brian.
They looked scared; and I thought they had every right
to be. For Brian still stood like a statue, head, shoulders,
arms rigid, radiating shame and fury.

At last he spoke.

'Where's Kenny? Where is he?'

It was a voice to send shivers down the spine. It sent
them down mine, and then back up again, until I could
feel the hairs on my neck rising one by one. Frank mumbled
unhappily. Brian shook his head.

'I'll break him in two, Frank,' he murmured. 'I
will.'

'But –' Lawrence bravely stood forward. 'Mr Hughes
liked it –'

John quickly hushed his friend, and pulled him away.
Between them, they got Lawrence's guitar back in its
case, and fastened the clasps. Then, easing their way
around Brian, as if he was an unexploded bomb and
they no heroes, they went their separate ways to where

each had left off work. Almost soundlessly, they began again counting the contents of the boxes.

Brian stayed where he was, near the sacks. Head down now, fists clenched. There was a deep silence in the warehouse.

A minute or so passed, and then I saw Kenny sidling into the room. Kenny's eyes were fixed on Brian. Brian didn't stir. Kenny took a tremulous couple of steps towards him.

'I heard he come up,' Kenny faltered.

No movement from Brian. Kenny glanced over at John, who nodded to confirm that indeed Mr Hughes had come up. Kenny advanced a little further towards Brian.

'I was havin' a shit, Bri.'

'Were you?' said Brian in a conversational voice.

'Yeah. I was.'

'Did you tell anybody else to keep a look-out while you were away?' Brian asked, in the same faintly interested tones.

There was a pause.

'No,' Kenny said at last.

'No. Well, you'd better go for a walk now, hadn't you?'

Brian crossed over the space between him and Kenny with lightning speed. He got hold of Kenny's shoulders and ran him up the gangway, all the way to the back of the room, where the loading bay gaped on to the open sky. There he took his hands away.

Kenny seemed a little puzzled as to why they had made this short excursion. Brian was feeling about now among the ropes and pulleys that hung at the side of the bay.

'I'm really sorry, Brian,' Kenny said, after watching the other for a while. 'I never thought the silly old c—t would –'

'Hold on to this.'

Kenny took the proffered rope. Stared at it. Then looked up at Brian.

'What –?'

'Now say thank you.'

'What for?'

"Cause I just saved your life,' said Brian.

And he put his hands on Kenny's narrow chest and gave a great push. Kenny hadn't time even to scream as he rocketed towards the open bay. We saw the body in motion – and then there was no more Kenny.

Brian, his task done, walked a little way away from the loading bay, and stood there, arms folded, looking thoughtful.

The rest of us were immobilised with shock. From where I was, I could see that both boys were frozen in the attitudes they were in when Brian began his running of Kenny towards the bay. I didn't turn to see what Frank was doing. I couldn't, couldn't move at all. But there was no sound from the desk. No sound anywhere. The seconds ticked away. I stared at the empty bay, the blank white sky.

And then we heard, just faintly, a cry for help. It brought the boys to life. They rushed over to the bay, leaned perilously over the ledge.

'He's hanging on!' John called out.

And now, stronger, came the cries from below the bay.

'Bri! Help me! Help me!'

I watched as Brian shook his head dourly. He said then, almost to himself, 'Why should I, Kenny?'

The boys looked round at him. It was clear they didn't know what to do. They peered down again at the hapless victim.

51

'He can't hold on much longer,' Lawrence cried.

'Stupid bastards!'

We all looked round at that. It was Frank, and yet for once an entirely comprehensible Frank. He was on his feet. He was moving down the gangway, as fast as ever I'd seen him move, except a couple of times when Kenny had especially startled him. He shouldered the boys out of the way, and got hold of the rope. Staunchly he pulled on it, and after a time a frantic and bloody face rose into view. The boys leaned out and got hold of the arms. Slowly Kenny was hoisted to safety.

Brian shook his head once again.

'It's all very well, Frank,' he sighed. 'But I'll have to do it eventually.'

II

1

After the traumas of their first day, the boys settled down quite happily into our little community on the sixth floor. And I ought to say here perhaps that although a narrative such as this is likely to concentrate *on* such traumas, they were not after all that characteristic of our life in the warehouse. Which in general proceeded at its habitual sleepy, near snail-like pace. Set against the few moments of upheaval and violence – always precipitated by a visit from Kenny – were the long calm hours of conversation, reflection, and steady labour. Time on the sixth floor always had for me a dreamlike, expansive quality. Days were weeks, weeks months, a year like an epoch. Not that I mean time hung heavy on our hands up there. Uniquely, out of all the jobs I have ever done, I felt no temptation at all in this one towards clock-watching. Rather, time in the warehouse was like a daze from which one emerged at intervals, to shake oneself, to spend the few paltry hours away at home, or getting there, or getting back, before immersing oneself gladly again in that smooth, widening, trance-inducing pool.

I know that my own frailties at the time made me particularly susceptible to such perceptions – if time could stand still, what need was there for me ever to contemplate rejoining real life again? But I think even the boys, for all their natural liveliness, felt something of this. Of life having slowed down, grown at the edges in a strange, immeasurable fashion. So that although they were only to be with us for a little while, a fortnight or perhaps a bit longer, one almost could see the warehouse – the people, the tiers of shelves and the boxes, the loading window, the very air itself – seeping into their consciousnesses, and I guessed that their time here would grow and grow in their memories so that one day, looking back, it would seem like another life entirely they had once lived.

They were both likeable lads, who were not at all afraid of hard work. This latter quality was important in gaining them acceptance from Brian and Frank. If I have given the impression that little serious work got done in the warehouse, then I have been at fault. Though Brian worried constantly about the shrinking volume of orders that came up from the offices each day, in fact there was still usually more than enough to keep the two of them at full stretch. Often they could have used an extra stockman, but it was a point of pride between them that they would handle the whole thing by themselves. And I think it was an element in the moral superiority the sixth floor exerted over the rest of the building that, while we – or rather, while Brian and Frank were permanently under pressure and occasionally forced to perform heroic feats of labour, down below, in the offices, the personnel were so thick on the ground that, individually, they had hardly anything to do most of the time.

So the boys' industriousness, helping as it did to keep up the tone and character of the sixth floor, definitely recommended them, along with their other attractive qualities. Of the two, it was Lawrence who was the general favourite. He was a nice, straightforward kid, with a very

56

open, charming quality about him. He was easier to talk with, laughed more readily, was just more winning than his friend. Brian, who for most of the year exhibited a high degree of taciturnity, opened up surprisingly readily to young Lawrence. Often, as I crouched low among the shelves, I could hear the two of them chatting and laughing away like old mates. John too sometimes got into these conversations, but still I could see that Brian became most expansive and good-humoured when he and Lawrence were alone.

It was for the change they had wrought in Brian's usual unforthcoming mode that I most welcomed the boys' presence. Now that I think about it, this uncommunicative quality of his was probably a largely enforced one – given the nature of those he had to work beside. People, and not only Kenny, quite often visited the warehouse from the lower floors, and at those times – except with Kenny – Brian proved perfectly ready to talk. But those visits occupied only a small fraction of any one day. The rest of the time, there was just Frank and me. Virtually useless, in our respective ways. The boys, however, offered real scope, and Brian took advantage of it. It was a new ingredient in the charm the warehouse had for me. So good to hear Brian opening up, responding to their youth and high spirits, above all to their obvious admiration for him.

I – silently – applauded this admiration for, as I have said, I shared it to a high degree. And yet, I see I may not have given any clear indication why this should have been so. Leaping about the warehouse like a springbok each morning and afternoon, having an eccentric way with a ballad, throwing a fellow-worker out of a sixth-floor loading bay – all these do not add up, I know, to an entire portrait of a hero. Yet, I insist, it was in just such a way that

I had come to think of Brian. I wish now I could point to a single action of his, or a saying, that would prove his status beyond a doubt. I can't do it. Either my memory is at fault or, more likely, the reason is that his status could never be encapsulated so neatly. What I come back to always is the fact of his authority. The whole building recognised it, even Mr Hughes, even – with frantic disaffection – Kenny. The visitors that came up to the sixth floor, though they appeared for a variety of ostensible reasons connected with the work, almost always turned out at last to be seeking something from Brian: his advice, his opinion, his sympathy, his blessing. In most of the disputes and misunderstandings, personal and work-related, that arose at Hughes & Hughes, Brian ended up being the unofficial arbiter. And – at least until this Christmas – it was almost unthinkable that any major change in the way things were done, anywhere in the building, should take place without Brian's consent. I remember when a new lunch-hour rota for the junior office staff was issued from Mr Hughes' office. Officially it had nothing at all to do with Brian – and yet that rota did not go into effect until Brian, after a few days' consideration, had given his OK. He had authority.

As for what that authority rested upon – again I doubt if I can give a conclusive explanation, just as I never understood how exactly it operated on myself. I can list his qualities: his intelligence, a physical presence and attractiveness that amounted to glamour, that Stakhanovite capacity for hard work that made the rest of us feel fairly small. I can proceed from that last point to the fact that, in a real sense, most of us at Hughes & Hughes were rather puny characters, who looked for and rejoiced to find in Brian the strength and sureness that we lacked. In my own case, after my recent troubles, I knew

58

this was so to an exaggerated degree. All this was going on, yes, and yet I still don't feel it completely explains his authority, or accounts for it. Most of all it must have depended on Brian's own certainties. He seemed to accept and use that authority with complete assurance, like a king. It is true that, as far as the company as a whole was concerned, it was Mr Hughes who occupied the figurehead post of monarch, which made Brian more like the power behind the throne. The Grand Vizier. Or like one of those sergeant-majors who really runs the regiment whatever the useless colonel thinks. But on the sixth floor, I insist, his authority was not even diminished to that extent. He was our king, securely so as if descended from a long true line. And given that regal certitude, how was it possible for the rest of us – who were all really, from Mr Hughes down to myself, of unregenerate peasant stock – to dare to doubt, let alone to challenge his right to rule? Anyway, why should we? We had the luck to be ruled by a perfectly benevolent despot. Only a fool would want to see the end of this happy state. It would go on until the king himself should choose to step down, not a day before.

I see now that this was my delusion; it was not necessarily Brian's. I had not thought the termites could possibly yet have burrowed so deep. I hardly knew they had got started. But I think that Brian, who was shrewder than the rest of us, had been attentive to the approach of their hungry little jaws for some long time.

2

It was early one afternoon, four or five days after the boys had joined us. The weather had turned suddenly mild. A great shaft of sunlight carved through the air, from the loading bay deep into the warehouse. I had been feather-dusting on a high shelf and was now taking a short rest, watching the motes of dust I had stirred up as they drifted slowly down the edges of the light. Brian and Lawrence were on the other side of the tier I was working on. Brian had already finished the afternoon's orders – there hadn't been many at all today – and had come over to give Lawrence a hand with the inventory. He was up among the shelves counting, Lawrence was down below writing in the numbers that were called out. John wasn't around. He'd been lent to the stationery department for a couple of hours, to help stack away some new stock. Over at the desk Frank was leafing slowly through the slim pile of invoices. When he reached the end, he started at the top again, and he did this over and over, as if finally the pile would crack under his tireless stirring and yield up at last one still-unfilled order. Or perhaps, I thought, dreaming as I watched him, he is hoping that if he waits long enough and fiddles with it sufficiently, the pile will start breeding for him.

The counting on the other side of the tier had grown desultory, and Brian and Lawrence had fallen into a relaxed, discursive conversation, conducted mainly by Brian. I could hear them perfectly; and when I had adjusted a couple of boxes on the shelf before me, I could see them too. Brian was perched up on the fifth level of the far tier; Lawrence was standing, leaning against the tier opposite him, behind which, though invisible to them, I was able to sit and watch. Their voices as they talked were low and calm and unforced. It was a lazy, mellow afternoon; so quiet and settled, it was hard to imagine it ever ending. With any luck, I remember myself thinking, eternity will be like this.

'No,' I heard Brian say at one point, 'there's only three places in London where I would consider taking a shit.'

He yawned and dropped the last of the nuts he'd been counting back into its box.

'Fourteen doz . . . yeah, just the three. My place. My mum's place. And the club. Nowhere else.'

'You wouldn't go here?' Lawrence enquired.

'Never!'

Brian brooded for a moment, and then he dropped down from the shelf to land lightly on the floor. His face had grown dark and strained. And I felt uneasily that the afternoon had stirred suddenly from its trance, and that time was picking up its pace again.

'People like Kenny go here. You heard him the other day: "I was having a shit, Bri . . ." No –' Brian screwed up his fine dark eyes into angry slits. 'I wouldn't go anywhere near where that twisted, disgusting, degenerate little –'

He stopped himself then, perhaps recognising from the way Lawrence was staring at him that he was getting carried away. He reached into his overalls and took out

61

his Senior Service. He gave one to Lawrence. Then he said, with a trace of apology in his voice:

'We've had a pretty bad year, Kenny and me.'

He flicked a book-match against the emery paper, and held it to Lawrence's cigarette, then his own. Before he extinguished the flame, he looked into the boy's eyes.

'Has he talked to you about the union yet?'

Lawrence, surprised by the question – it had come at him almost like an accusation – coughed over his cigarette.

'What?' he said, when he'd recovered.

'You sure?'

'I don't know what you're talking about.'

Brian watched him for a moment or two more. The match flame neared his thumb and he blew it out. He nodded, satisfied.

'Never mind,' he said.

He moved along the tier a little way, and climbed up to the top shelf. Lawrence too shifted himself a few paces until he was again standing directly under Brian.

'What's his job?' he asked suddenly.

'Huh?'

'Kenny. What does he do?'

'Ah . . .' Looking down, Brian shook his head. 'Hasn't got a job really . . . Frank,' he called. 'What's Kenny doing nowadays?'

'Nu'un,' Frank called back.

'Nothing,' Brian nodded. 'I think that's about right. They wouldn't let him go out on the van any more. Not after the boy in Croydon. And nobody else wants him around.'

'Boy in Croydon?'

'Yup. This kid was standing at a zebra. Kenny drove up on the pavement and knocked him down. Broke his leg.'

'God!'

'He got off,' Brian said regretfully. 'Said it was an accident, his foot slipped. But it wasn't true. I heard him boasting about it.'

'But why –'

'He thought this kid was looking at him funny. Twelve years old . . . So now Kenny's just sort of on the strength. I give him a few odd jobs once in a while. Most of the time he don't do a stroke. It just wants somebody to tip Hughes off.' Brian nodded to himself. 'After Christmas . . .' he added thoughtfully.

He began counting the items in one of the boxes. Lawrence was standing in such a way that I could see his face in profile. It was apparent that some sort of struggle was taking place within him. At last he spoke up with a kind of faltering bravery.

'I didn't think – er – the other day . . . you should have actually . . . well, I just don't, you see . . .'

Brian stared down at him.

'What's up?'

'The loading bay,' said Lawrence, quite firmly. 'That was sort of dangerous. You could have killed him,' he added solemnly.

Brian went back to his counting.

'Mind your own business,' he said.

The boy bowed his head, sufficiently crushed. After a while, Brian looked down at him again. He hesitated, feeling – I guessed – that it was well beneath his dignity to offer an explanation. But in the end he sighed and said:

'Look. If I'd wanted to knock him off, I wouldn't do it that way . . . I gave him a rope, didn't I?' Brian argued defensively. 'Kenny's like a little cat, all arms and legs. I knew he'd hang on.'

'His nose is all busted up,' said Lawrence, still daring.

'Oh, what a shame!' Brian gazed at the boy. 'Well, I'm glad to see he's got one friend in the world anyway.'

'I didn't mean –' Lawrence began hastily.

'He does have one or two little faults you ought to know about if you're gonna be his pal. However, it's up to you.'

After a final irritated glance, Brian turned again to the box. He was clearly much offended. Lawrence stared up worriedly at his rigid, affronted back. Brian ran quickly through the remainder of the box's contents.

'Hundred twenty-six,' he reported shortly. He jumped again from the high shelf, landing this time with quite a noisy impact.

'There. Finny. That's enough for me.'

Without looking at Lawrence, he strolled towards the desk, taking his crimson bandana off as he went.

'Come and have a pint,' he said to Frank.

Frank willingly heaved himself to his feet. He took his muffler from a drawer in the table. Then looked to where Lawrence had emerged from the gangway and was standing, watching them. Frank pointed at the boy.

'Wha 'bou' . . .?'

'No,' said Brian coldly. 'He stays here.'

Lawrence looked so rejected and depressed my heart went out to him. And I suppose even Brian felt some pity for him, for just before he went out the door he looked back and called in a not-unfriendly voice:

'Hold the fort then, Lawrence.'

3

The men were gone. Lawrence sighed. And then turned and went, head bowed, towards a box on a bottom shelf, near the gangway. He sat down in front of it. I watched him sitting there, thinking. After a while, he pulled the box out, and began counting the three-inch nails inside.

There was a faint sound from the doorway. Lawrence looked around eagerly, no doubt hoping that Brian, relenting, had come back to ask him to join them in the pub. Or at least that John, having finished his work downstairs, had returned to keep him company. But I saw that immediately after Lawrence had looked towards the door an expression of surprise, then alarm, then almost of horror came over his face. His jaw dropped. I craned my neck to see what had caused this transformation.

Kenny had arrived. He had come a little way into the room. On his pale face, across the bridge of his nose, was a wide, grubby sticking-plaster. He had been wearing this – flaunting it, like a badge of courage or protest – since the afternoon Brian had sent him out of the loading bay. I happened to know it was only a decoration by now, for I had seen him remove it for a few seconds in the third-floor lavatory, and there was now nothing underneath but a slight graze. It was certainly not this which had brought such dread to Lawrence's normally cheerful features. No, that clearly had been caused by the sight of what Kenny was carrying, loosely, across his arms.

'Where's Brian?' Kenny said flatly.

Lawrence could do nothing but stare at the rifle.

'I got somethin' for him,' said Kenny in the same parched, deadly tone.

Lawrence, by dint of swallowing several times, managed to clear his throat at last.

'He's out,' he croaked from between whitened lips.

At that, Kenny relaxed. He slung the rifle under his arm, whipped out a small mirror from the inside pocket of the blue-stripe seersucker jacket he was wearing that day.

'Look at my *face*!' he cried out, turning his head this way and that the better to appreciate the heroic glamour of his Elastoplasted nose.

Lawrence rose from his sitting position, tentatively approached Kenny. He kept his eyes all the while on the weapon that protruded from under Kenny's arm.

'What's that?' he asked in a hushed voice.

''S my Webley,' said Kenny proudly. He became animated. Tucked away his mirror. Showed Lawrence the air-gun. 'It's got a great range,' he boasted. 'Here . . .'

He led Lawrence over to the loading bay. I was impressed that after his recent experience he could go up to it so casually. The thrill of the hunt must have been in him, dispelling all other thoughts. He stuck his hand into his pocket and brought out a slug. Broke open the gun and fitted it into the barrel. He stared keenly out of the window, towards the roofs on the other side of Cutt Street.

'There!' he cried out. 'See that one? With the stripey tail?'

He raised the rifle-butt to his shoulder, took quick

66

aim. Before Lawrence could make a move, he fired. A loud report. Then a second later, a high shriek of feline pain from somewhere beyond the bay. Kenny laughed uproariously and felt for another slug. Lawrence stared out of the bay mournfully.

'He's just stunned a bit,' Kenny explained. 'See him wriggle?'

He put the rifle up to his shoulder again.

'Stop it!'

Lawrence grabbed Kenny's arm as he fired. I guessed it must have made him miss, not just because the cat didn't scream this time – the poor beast may have been past screaming – but because Kenny was so furious.

'Oy!' he shouted, and he turned and clipped Lawrence smartly across the head. 'What d'you think you're doin', c—t?'

He raised his hand for another swipe. Lawrence back-pedalled away from him fast. Kenny followed him down the gangway, flailing out with his free fist. Halfway down, Lawrence turned and broke away, diving for a tier of shelves. He scrambled up to the top, Kenny still hard on his heels. I too was dodging from tier to tier, trying to keep them in view. I saw Lawrence go right over the top. He plunged down towards the pile of sacks below, that podium from which, the other day, he and John had failed disastrously to entertain us. He landed heavily on the sacks and sprawled there, somewhat winded. Kenny, still carrying the air-gun, leaped down and landed right on top of him.

Lawrence struggled underneath. Kenny, laughing now rather wildly, kept him pressed down upon the sacks. Suddenly, Lawrence gave up. He lay still. On top of him, Kenny too stopped struggling.

A moment passed, another, another. I saw then Kenny reach his free hand between the boy's legs.

'NO, KENNY!'

Lawrence shouted and he fought like a wildcat. He wriggled out from under Kenny, who then sprang to his feet, laughing again, squealing with panicky glee.

'You'd better not tell anyone,' Kenny said. He'd stopped laughing by now. He had backed against a tier and was watching Lawrence with angry, uncertain eyes. Lawrence was climbing slowly to his feet.

'I tell you,' said Kenny grimly. 'You'd better *not* talk.'

Lawrence shook his head numbly.

Kenny pumped his gun open and shut.

'Otherwise . . . I could destroy your eyes.'

'It's all right,' Lawrence said. 'It's OK.'

He seemed to be recovering from his shock. In fact, I suspected that he now felt rather foolish at having drawn such marked attention to an incident that, if he'd shown more *savoir-faire*, could have been passed off as nothing at all really, just a bit of fun. However, that was impossible now, and it seemed to me that Lawrence, recognising this, was determined at least to put the unhappy situation to some good use. He was a very moral boy, very concerned about the large number of public evils that raged unchecked in the world. Up here on the sixth floor he had already regaled us – somewhat to his friend John's embarrassment – with a number of passionate attacks on various contemporary crimes: the bad racial situation in the southern United States, in South Africa, the mounting crisis in Vietnam, etc., etc. Brian and Frank listened to all this as if it was news from another planet, though I could see that Brian was impressed at least by the boy's fervour, and range of information, and

68

generous, indignant sympathies on behalf of so many disadvantaged groups around the world. All this was now to be gathered up and focused on the delicate case of Kenny.

'You're not to worry,' Lawrence said kindly. (I saw Kenny take a firmer grip upon his rifle.) 'That sort of thing . . .' The boy hesitated. Then: 'Well, it's not for me, sorry. Not that it disgusts me, or anything,' he added hastily. 'It's just . . . But anyway, *I* believe –' His voice was ringing out now in a tone of exalted conviction. 'That no matter what anyone says, people like you – *homosexuals* – have a perfect right to –'

Kenny fired.

4

Lawrence screamed. I saw him clap hands to his eyes. He dropped to his knees.

'I'm blind!'

I heard Lawrence wailing, I heard Kenny roaring with laughter. I was so shocked at what had happened that, without thinking, I actually took a step out of my hiding-place and towards the gangway. I knew I had to do something – but it was so long since I'd done anything that had to do with other people . . . I didn't know what I was going to do.

John saved me. He must have been coming up the stairs, and had heard Lawrence's screams all the way down there, for he came racing into the room, crying out:

'What's happening?'

Kenny laughed even more uproariously. John ran up to Lawrence and prised his hands away from his face. There was not a mark on it, and I remembered at last that Kenny hadn't reloaded his rifle since his second shot at the cat.

Still, it had come as a great shock for Lawrence. He crouched there on the sacks, his face back in his hands, gulping back sobs. John looked down at him unhappily, then at Kenny.

'You rotten sod.'

Kenny stopped laughing. Stared coldly at John. Then broke open his gun. He reached into his pocket and abstracted another slug. Fitted it in. Snapped the barrel shut.

'You said what?'

John hesitated. He sorely wanted to have a go at Kenny, I could see. On the other hand, Kenny was holding the gun now in just the position he'd aimed it at Lawrence. From such a range, even an air-gun slug could do some nasty damage.

'Go on – who are you calling a sod, you c—t?'

I could see that Kenny was working himself up. I was praying that John would back down. Yet I already knew – from one or two lively spats he had got into with Brian over the past few days – that John had a temper in him, and, unfortunately, courage. He glanced down again at his friend's white, wretched face. Then he looked back at Kenny, stared at him unflinching, and stated at last:

'You. You're the sod.'

And I don't know what would have happened if Brian and Frank hadn't returned at that moment. We all looked round at them. Brian stood stock-still for a moment, sizing up the situation – Kenny and John, Lawrence's distraught face, the rifle. Then he walked directly towards Kenny.

'Don't pull him up this time, Frank.'

Kenny dropped the rifle. He backed away from Brian. His hand scrambled into his inside pocket.

'I brought you something, Bri,' he cried out.

He held out an envelope in one shaking hand. Brian stopped. Studied it.

'It's your girl-friend,' said Kenny, breathing easier. A confidential tone had entered his voice. 'She gave it to Hoover. Hoover gave it to me.'

71

Brian took the letter out of Kenny's hand. It seemed to signal the end of the immediate crisis. I could see that Kenny was all at once thoroughly relaxed. He even leered a little as Brian slit the envelope open with his forefinger.

'Young Daphne . . .'

Brian regarded him briefly. I thought he would surely want to chastise such cheek, such *lèse-majesté*. Instead he only said, quite gently:

'Dorothy.'

John was kneeling down in front of Lawrence and asking him if he was all right. Lawrence was nodding, yes, OK. He was clearly rather ashamed by now to have made such a fuss. He was still obviously shaken up though. Kenny ignored both boys. He had his eyes on Brian all the time. Brian read his letter. A couple of times he chuckled to himself. Kenny smirked pruriently.

'What is it? . . . Go on, Bri.'

Brian looked up at Kenny in disgust. Then he folded the letter, put it back in its envelope, stuffed it into the pocket of his jacket.

'Go away, Kenny,' he said.

He strolled back to the desk then, removed the jacket and hung it up. Pulled the tin full of goo towards him. Got a dab of it on his palm, and began to rub it in.

Kenny, as disregarded as if he'd been an insect, shrugged and stooped over to pick up his rifle.

'Leave it there,' Brian said, still not looking at Kenny.

For a moment it looked as if Kenny would try to disobey. But he thought the better of it. Rifleless, he slunk angrily from the room. Brian didn't glance at him as he went by. He finished applying the cream to his palms, then walked back to the middle of the gangway and kicked the air-gun into a far corner. He looked down at Lawrence then. Contemplated him with a caustic gleam in his eyes.

'Nice of Kenny to drop in, wasn't it?'

But watching Lawrence, his mockery subsided. He looked quite concerned now.

'You all right?' he asked at length.

Lawrence nodded. Then he heaved himself up and moved slowly to the box where he'd been counting in that distant age before Kenny came in. He certainly looked to me like somebody who had grown a great deal older within that passage of time. Brian watched him go, then looked at John.

'What happened?'

John shrugged. Brian scowled.

'I'm gonna see that little bugger out of here.'

He stood thinking for a moment longer, then with a shake of his head dismissed the episode.

'Right, I want a hand. Get hold of that.'

He pointed to the loading-trolley. John went and seized the handle and pushed it towards Brian who led him over to a tier. He pointed up to a high shelf.

'There's some heavy old brackets up there . . .'

'I'll get 'em.'

John put his hands on the lower shelf, was starting to climb. Brian stopped him.

'No, you won't. Got to be careful, your age. Don't want a rupture.' He started climbing up. 'You hold still. I'll pass 'em down.'

On the desk the telephone rang. Frank ignored it. Brian dropped to the floor, went over and picked it up. He listened. Frowned.

'What for?'

He listened again.

'All right.'

He hung up. Looked at Frank, puzzled.

'Kenny . . . Says Hughes wants to see me.'

73

Frank wasn't able to shed any light on this, so Brian shrugged and quit the room. John, rather pleased, I thought, that he'd been left to do the heavy, important work, shinned up his tier and started extracting brackets from the box. The afternoon fell into place. Frank was studying his invoices, Lawrence was very quietly and slowly inventorying. John was working like a beaver.

At this point, I saw Kenny stealthily re-entering the warehouse.

5

I imagine he had mainly come back to retrieve his air-gun. He walked up and down the gangway, evidently looking for something. It appeared then as if he wanted to put the question to us, where was the weapon? But it was equally evident, as he looked at each of the three visible occupants of the warehouse in turn, that none of them would divulge its location. So like some angry little missile diverted from its main target, Kenny turned towards a secondary one. He hurried over towards the desk and, easily dodging the lumbering blows that Frank aimed at him, he snatched the envelope from the pocket of Brian's jacket. He skipped into the middle of the gangway, taking the letter out of its envelope as he went. The boys in spite of themselves couldn't help looking up and taking an interest. I was in the same position.

'"My darling, darling Brian . . ."' Kenny read out.

I could see the writing. The ink was of a vivid, almost violent shade of green. The writing childishly round and loopy. The paper was lined, had two holes in it along the margin. It looked to have been removed from a school ring-book.

Kenny looked up at us, leering. 'The f——r! Fourteen years old. A f——n' schoolgirl!' He went back to the letter.

'Here. Listen to this. "I'm writing this in my bedroom. I wish so much you were here, Bri. Last night I had such a lovely dream about us. We'd gone out in the country on your bike. And we were stopped in a wood. And you asked me to take off all my – "'

Kenny read on silently now, his lips moving as he deciphered each word, his eyes bulging.

'*Dirty* little cow!'

He looked up triumphantly. Waved the letter before him.

'I could put him inside with this.'

'You wouldn't,' John cried out, aghast.

'Why not?' Kenny raged. 'He's a f——n' lunatic. You saw what he done to me.' He gestured furiously at the open loading bay. Then went back to the letter. Laughed coarsely.

'"Now I'm writing in Geography. I hate it. I wish I was with you. I'm getting really excited thinking about what we could be doing. Remember when I came to your flat that first time and I said I didn't mind, you could do anything at all to me. Anything you wanted. That's the way I'm feeling now, Bri. I'm so wet – "'

While he read, Kenny was moving excitedly about. As he came near the desk, Frank made a lunge for the letter.

'Gi'i' back,' he groaned.

'Shut up, moron,' Kenny snarled, moving fast away from Frank. He shook the letter above his head. 'That bent c—t! I'm tellin' you, boys, I could have him with this. I could – '

There was a thunder of footsteps on the stairs. And then came Brian's voice roaring for blood.

'Kenny! Where are you, Kenny?'

Kenny looked around wildly. Then he dived at where

the sacks lay piled up. He wriggled his way underneath the first few layers.

'Hide me!' he implored. 'Hide me.'

The footsteps were pounding ever closer. The two boys looked at each other. And then Lawrence got up and went over to the sacks and tried to cover Kenny's quivering form.

I was so struck by his action, considering earlier events. An imitation of Christ almost, it seemed to me. Forgive them that persecute you, etc. However, it wasn't of much practical avail. Kenny's high-heeled Chelsea boots were still sticking out from under the hessian, clearly visible.

Brian came into the room in a terrible anger.

'Where is he? I know he's here.'

He paced along the gangway. He came to the recess where the sacks were. Those mod-boots were in motion before him, as Kenny shook in his terror.

Brian studied this spectacle for a long moment. Even in his fury he couldn't help grinning. He turned away then, and I thought Kenny must have escaped his wrath after all. Kenny, not knowing what was happening above him, couldn't restrain himself from giving a low moan of fearful anticipation.

I saw then that Brian had only turned away in order to gather himself for his vengeance. He turned back now, his handsome features dark with rage. He reached down to tear the sacks from the helpless, guilty, soon-to-be horribly punished body.

At that moment, the phone rang again. Brian hesitated. For once Frank – who evidently wanted execution to proceed on Kenny without interruption – chose to pick up the phone. He listened. And then held it out to Brian. Brian looked regretfully down at the mound of sacks. Then sighed, returned to the desk, took the phone from Frank's great paw.

'Yeah?'

A puzzled frown grew on his brow. I saw that Kenny, looking almost as shaken as Lawrence had a while ago, had crawled out from under the sacks, and was climbing to his feet. He still had the letter crumpled up in one hand, and as I watched I saw him drop it into his jacket pocket.

'Now?' said Brian into the phone. Then he shrugged. 'OK.'

He hung up. Turned to the rest of us. Kenny took a step backward. But Brian seemed to have lost interest in him.

'It really was Hughes this time,' he said thoughtfully. 'Wants to see us.'

There was a pause. Then Kenny asked:

'All of us?'

'Everyone except the boys.'

He looked at Frank. Frank shrugged.

'What's goin' on?' Kenny asked.

Brian stared at him.

'What've you been up to?'

'Nothin'!' cried Kenny, outraged.

There did seem to be a certain note of innocence in Kenny's voice, the more striking because so rarely heard. Brian shook his head again, clearly baffled by this general summons. Then he turned and left the room. Frank got up and went after him. Kenny stayed where he was for a moment, but in the end his curiosity overcame his anxiety. He followed the other two. The boys, suddenly abandoned, looked at each other, both equally at sea.

And I, for the second time that day, felt impelled to get mixed up in the excitements and confusions of life. And this time I did something about it. I put down my duster and headed directly for the door.

6

Though I was very aware of how uncharacteristic and unprecedented was this move of mine, it didn't seem to impress itself greatly on my co-workers when I joined them downstairs in the line that had formed up in front of Mr Hughes' desk. They were too occupied with staring at our employer as, self-consciously, he sat leafing through a pile of papers before him, occasionally adding a note in their margins with a gold-nibbed fountain-pen. When eventually he looked up, his gaze travelled along our line. I saw some uncertainty creep into his eyes as, at the last, they rested on me. I could understand it. I don't think Mr Hughes and I had exchanged a word since the day, two years ago, that he'd hired me. But he quickly dismissed whatever questions my presence posed him. He had more important things on his mind. His face grew long, momentous, mournful – and yet I thought I saw traces of excitement and anticipation lurking there too.

'This is a sad moment for me,' Mr Hughes intoned at last. 'A sad, sad moment.'

And as if the sorrow had become all at once too much for him, he looked away from us. Kenny shuffled unhappily on the spot beside me. I could not see what the others were doing. Continuing to stare at the managing director, I supposed. He presented certainly a more compelling picture than one's usual sight of him pottering dreamily around the building. The whole scene before us was calculated to impress. The great desk with its towering piles of documents and correspondence. The deep leather armchair in which Mr Hughes sat. The mahogany panelling behind him. The portraits of his predecessors that lined the walls. I noticed that several of these shared the protuberant eyes and rather weak smile that characterised their descendant here before us. But some of them, particularly the Victorian ones, glowered down from their frames in a properly stern and forbidding fashion. Everything fitted precisely into this scene, just as if it had all been chosen by a conscientious set-designer. It must have been that which gave the present moment its slight air of staginess.

Mr Hughes sighed heavily, and forced himself to look at us again.

'I've been comparing the inventory figures as they've been coming down from the warehouse against our sales receipts for the year.' He stopped. Shook his head, slowly, impressively. 'I find there are very grave discrepancies.'

Silence. A clock ticked. A girl laughed in a nearby office.

Kenny burst out suddenly:

'It's them boys. They don't know what they're doin'.'

Mr Hughes shook his head again, sorrowful lines etched his forehead.

'I don't think we can shift the blame on to the boys,' he said.

Another silence. Then Brian stirred.

'It's a fact, Mr Hughes. The boys . . . well, they try hard, but they don't always get it right.'

For a third time, Mr Hughes set his head rocking from

80

side to side in pained regret. I couldn't help thinking he was enjoying himself tremendously.

'I only wish it were that simple. But you see, Brian –' Here he allowed himself to smile proudly. 'For the past couple of nights, after you've all gone home, I've been up on the sixth floor checking the inventory myself.'

After a moment, Brian said coolly:

'Have you?'

'Yes. I have. I found . . . certain trifling errors in the boys' work. But nothing that would explain *this*.'

He picked up a sheet of paper from the desk. Fitted a pair of half-moon spectacles to his nose.

'For instance – split cotter pins. Our sales figures show we should have eleven and a half gross left in stock. We have less than a gross. Over ten gross are not accounted for . . . Again – half-inch Bedfords – five gross are missing. And so it goes on. And what they indicate,' concluded Mr Hughes, 'I'm sorry to say, is a record of massive, systematic theft from the warehouse, extending back –' He shrugged. 'I don't know how far back. Certainly long before the boys joined us. Which means that the range of suspects is necessarily pretty narrow.'

His gaze swept over us again. And then seemed to settle firmly upon Kenny. Who immediately became agitated.

'I ain't done nothin'!' he cried.

Mr Hughes continued to study him. I could feel Kenny shaking in his boots beside me.

'I don't want yer rotten nuts and bolts,' he quavered, in a very Kenny-like mixture of fury and fear. And then, as Mr Hughes' gaze still fastened on him, he turned in panic for help.

'Brian!'

Thus appealed to, Brian took a step forward.

'You sure about all this, Mr Hughes?' he asked quietly.

For answer, Mr Hughes tossed the paper across the desk.

'See for yourself,' he sighed.

Brian picked up the sheet and appeared to study it. I guessed that he was playing for time. I was very worried, for I knew exactly who the culprit was. Though my existence on the sixth floor was so shadowy, and I seemed to play no part at all in its unfolding story, it was my pride that nothing that happened up there ever escaped my notice. And I had been aware for a long time that Brian occasionally helped himself to small quantities of the stock. I believe he sold what he took to little shops around Kilburn where he lived. On the point of morality, it didn't bother me. He was paid so little for the great amount of work that he did, that it seemed to me only fair that he should supplement it in this way. And he was always generous with the extra money he got, he helped out other people, he was always good for a handsome donation to somebody's leaving present. No, I was not surprised, nor was I shocked to know that Brian was – to put it at its coarsest – a thief. It had certainly never affected my belief in his heroic stature, for example. Two things did puzzle me though at this moment. One was the size of the losses Mr Hughes had uncovered. I hadn't known Brian was making off with so much. Really it looked as if a small fortune had been passing through his hands. The other detail that surprised me was to find he had not managed to cover his traces better. I had been certain that Brian would have had the good sense to fiddle the stock-keeping entries if he was going to be making such inroads into the stock.

7

I watched Brian as he continued to study the figures on the paper in his hand. I felt more and more apprehensive. I had always thought that Brian was so deeply embedded in the world of Hughes & Hughes that, short of deliberately burning the building to the ground, he would never be in danger of losing his job. But stealing on this scale – I could not see how it could be forgiven. And even if he was allowed to stay, I could see that his position would be entirely different. Mr Hughes would permanently enjoy the moral whip-hand. Brian would be demoted, spiritually as well as in fact. His wings would be clipped. He would not be Brian any more.

I did not know which eventuality I most feared: that he should be fired, or that he should be diminished. Either was an unendurable prospect for anyone who was proud to be, however silently, a disciple of his, for anyone who counted on his powerful influence to keep everything ticking over at Hughes & Hughes, steady and tranquil and unchanging. I even thought of stepping forward and confessing to the crime myself. Only the fact that I was sure I would not be believed held me back. I also feared that they would probably all collapse laughing at the very idea of me showing enough initiative to mastermind such a major theft.

Mr Hughes meanwhile was still clearly relishing his own performance as Poirot. He had leaned back deep into his chair, and had placed his fingers together before him, so that the tips were just touching. Over these he continued to survey our little line-up of suspects. As before, his gaze was focused most often on the hapless Kenny.

'Now,' he began, 'I don't want to make a public spectacle of this. I'd like to keep the whole wretched business as private as possible. So I shan't ask the guilty party to own up at this point. But when the rest of you leave, I should like him to stay behind.'

Brian looked up briefly from the paper.

'That's not very private,' he said.

Mr Hughes considered this. A worried expression came over his mild features.

'I suppose not. What do you think we should do, Brian?'

Brian didn't answer at first. He laid the paper back on the desk. Stood thinking for a moment. Then said quietly:

'I should like to stay behind, Mr Hughes.'

For a second or two, Mr Hughes didn't seem to see what he was getting at. Then he understood. He was genuinely shocked.

'Brian!' he breathed.

Brian continued to stand there, ramrod-straight, gazing at a point on the wall just above Mr Hughes' head. I saw Frank and Kenny looking at him. Frank looked – not so surprised, but very worried. I guessed he knew as well as I did what Brian had been up to, and regretted like me that it had come to light. On Kenny's narrow little face, by contrast, there was a look of dawning glee.

Mr Hughes seemed not to know at first what to do or what to say.

'Well,' he faltered, 'er – yes . . . well . . .' He stared up at Brian as if hoping against hope that he would start to smile and confess that he'd been kidding. I saw now that Mr Hughes had not at all expected to land so big a fish, and was unsure how to handle it. Kenny was his target, and the extent of his hope had been that he could display unsuspected executive talent in rooting the mischief out. But as he watched Brian, I think certain other possibilities began to occur to him. He grew steadier in his gaze, and a rather hopeful, calculating look replaced the surprise and confusion that had first appeared in his eyes. I wondered if he had already seen how, with a judicious mixture of forgiveness and spite, he could at last reduce to manageable proportions that dominance of Brian's that had chafed him for so long.

'Very well,' said Mr Hughes, briskly now. He looked away from Brian. 'Well, thank you for coming down, Frank,' he said graciously. 'And – er –'

'Kenny,' said Kenny.

'Yes, I *know* that,' Mr Hughes said, somewhat querulously. 'Thank you, Kenny. And –' But he gave up entirely when he got to me. 'I'm sorry you all had to be placed in this very difficult –'

'Quite all right, Mr Hughes,' said Kenny jovially. 'Only too glad to be of assistance.'

And we the innocent trailed out of the office. Frank and I looked back sorrowfully at Brian, who still stood there before the desk, straight and unyielding. Kenny too looked back. The grin on his face was diabolical.

8

John and Lawrence were waiting for us out in the corridor.

'What's going on?' John asked as, in our different moods, we exited from the office.

'Shut up,' Kenny hissed. He got hold of the door handle and turned it gently. 'I can't miss this . . .' He chortled almost soundlessly. 'Thieving bastard!'

He pushed open the door an inch or two. We could see Brian still standing there, and Mr Hughes' hands on his desk as he toyed with a paper-knife. Kenny giggled.

Then, glancing round, he noticed me.

'F—k off, you,' he whispered furiously. 'Get out of here.'

I retired, but only to go a little way down the corridor. I could no longer see what was going on in the office, but I could hear the voices clear.

'Ah, Brian, Brian . . .' I heard Mr Hughes say. 'This is a tragedy.'

At the door, Kenny had to hold his hand against his mouth to stop himself laughing out loud. The others were watching with painful intensity. I crept a little closer to the door.

'How long have you been with us, Brian? Fifteen years, is it? Sixteen? Longer?'

Another step and I was just able to see through the crack again. Kenny was too intent on watching the scene to bother with me.

Mr Hughes sighed deeply.

'I little thought that one day –'

Brian stirred impatiently.

'Those figures don't add up,' he said.

'– I should have to talk to you in these unhappy circum—'

Mr Hughes' voice suddenly stopped. For several seconds there was silence. And then he said:

'What?'

'Have a look,' said Brian. He pushed the paper across the desk. Then he went round it to join Mr Hughes, and we could no longer see them. Kenny impatiently pushed the door open a few more inches. Brian was standing at Mr Hughes' side. He pointed down at the sheet of paper.

'There,' he said. 'Do that one.'

Mr Hughes stared up at Brian. And then, as ordered, picked up his fountain-pen and started on the sum. After a moment, Brian shook his head wearily.

'No, no. When you carry something you *add*, you don't take away. That's what you keep doing . . . Now start again.'

Mr Hughes went back to the beginning. He fumbled and scratched and crossed things out. After a little while, quite gently, Brian took the pen from his fingers. He finished the calculation rapidly.

'There you are, you see. You're just three out now. And that, I would think, is down to the boys.'

Mr Hughes sat staring down at the paper. I thought I had never seen anyone look so beaten.

'Want to try another one?' Brian asked.

At that point, not bothering to suppress the noise he made, Kenny slammed the door shut, and we saw no more.

'That stupid f——r!' Kenny fumed. 'Ignorant c—t!'

Frank, rendered extra-incomprehensible by relief and satisfaction, jeered at him triumphantly.

'Ah, piss off, half-wit!' Kenny roared, and turned away and – I swear – blinking back tears of rage, rushed off up the stairs. The boys and Frank were left grinning at each other. I knew I was grinning too but, wanting now that the crisis was over to disengage myself, I stepped back a few paces down the corridor, away from them.

Brian came out of the office then. He closed the door carefully behind him. Stood looking for a moment at the joyful faces before him. Then he glanced at the office door, shook his head.

'Poor old sod,' he sighed.

'You could sue him, Brian,' John said indignantly. 'It's slander, it's – you could *sue* him.'

Brian smiled.

'D'you reckon?'

'Definitely. You could get a lot of money.'

Brian seemed to take the notion seriously for a moment – but I was pretty certain he was only humouring John.

'Don't think the old fool's *got* a lot of money any more,' he said thoughtfully. He smiled again then. 'Nah, what I'll do, I'll just take the rest of the day off. I reckon I'm owed that . . . 'Night, boys, Frank.'

And Brian went off slowly down the corridor. He had his head down, thinking. He passed me without a glance. Frank started up the stairs. The boys looked at each other, and then, reluctantly, followed him. I was left alone in the corridor. Before I quitted it, I couldn't resist opening Mr Hughes' door once more.

He was still sitting at his desk. He had taken the fountain-pen into his hand again and, I supposed, had been trying to work at a few more sums, hoping against hope that one of them would come out right for him and prove that he was not a complete incompetent after all. That hope had died by now. He sat there, motionless, bent over the desk. The portraits of his ancestors stared down at him. I thought that even the silly-looking ones wore expressions of pained disgust at seeing to what a depth their race had sunk. It was a gloomy sight, and after a few seconds I was glad to shut the door on it.

III

1

When I was younger, about John and Lawrence's age, I used to work at holiday jobs too. It was customary then – I think it must have become much less so in subsequent decades, as unemployment spread. In those days, you went looking for work in about the last fortnight of the school term and, as every employer seemed to be short-staffed, if you had any persistence at all you were bound to find something. And for two or three weeks at Christmas and Easter, or for six weeks in the summer, you would have this other life – you would be a shop-assistant, or a milkman, or a postman, or dig potatoes, or pick peas, or serve behind the counter at a Lyons' Tea House, or wash the dishes there. You made a bit of money, enough to buy the new record-player, or a second-hand Lambretta, or a month on the road on the Continent next summer. And almost best of all, you would have numerous unfamiliar experiences on the job to offset the interminable irritations and tedium of everyday life at home or school. Even the worst jobs were of some use. I remember one I got in a factory where all I had to do was pull a lever all day long. After a few hours of this I was hallucinating in my despair. It was made very clear to me why it was a good idea to pass some exams and ensure that I never had to work at such a job as this for real, for life.

Sometimes on those holiday jobs I used to encounter men who, when I look back, though never of Brian's unique stature, bore a certain family resemblance to him. Clever men, of considerable personal force, working in very ordinary, even menial jobs. (I met even more women who were in that situation too but, in those days, theirs was obviously a different story.) I don't know whether such a phenomenon still holds good. Clearly it had to do with the old class system that assigned people to levels of work and authority without much regard to their native talents or potential, and that system is supposed to be much diluted and fractured now. Whatever the truth of that, in one way I think things have certainly changed, and that is in the degree of complacency with which such commanding characters would now accept their humble assignments. Though the routine of the warehouse often made Brian gloomy and prompted him to dream of escape, of cruise liners and the Seven Seas, still he never, as far as I could tell, experienced his life at Hughes & Hughes as a permanent, cruel insult. He had left school at fourteen or fifteen, had taken the first job that was offered and – save for a couple of years' gap in the Navy – here he still was after nearly two decades. And here he expected to stay. He never, in my hearing, spoke seriously of changing jobs. What would be the point given the status – if not the money or the title – that he enjoyed at Hughes & Hughes?

Also he never, I am certain, thought of not working – which, I suppose, would be a real alternative for a formidable person who finds himself stuck in a lousy job today. I look at somebody bright and articulate on TV now, a man or woman, black or white, of natural authority and intelligence, who refuses to work in a job that doesn't measure up to their talents, and I can certainly see their point of view. Brian would not have understood this attitude at all. In fact, I am sure he would have despised it.

In this, as in other ways, Brian at this time showed himself to be somewhat out of date. Perhaps just by a couple of years, at most half a dozen, but even so he was in the position very much of holding still while the world advanced around him. The spirit of gritty endurance, of bearing up and smiling through, the old Blitz spirit, fundamentally one of deference, however proudly, even aggressively, borne – Brian's spirit, in fact – had had its day. Many of those events that marked the end of the interminable English post-war period had happened by now. The Conservative government had been voted out, the Beatles had arrived, President Kennedy had been shot – a new day, as one of John and Lawrence's pithy folk songs might well have remarked, was dawning.

And to add to the list of momentous disrupting events that marked off the new era from what had gone before, Kenny had descended on the scene – or better: had risen up into the world of Hughes & Hughes as if through a trap-door from down below, like a demon in a pantomime. This was a restless, angry spirit, a spirit of novelty and change and destruction, and it lurked underneath us all the time, except when, every so often, it erupted among us, and seemed to threaten . . . well, all we had really: that compound of hard work and, occasionally, high spirits, and the long, busy, peaceful days. Frank in his baker's coat calling out the invoices, Brian reading aloud from the *Sketch*, the changing sky outside the loading bay, dreams of freedom, cosiness in the teeth of the blistering cold – everything that made a singular though familiar sense out of the daily round. And all under Brian's authority, where we sheltered, perfectly safe, safe (as it seemed to me, on days when I felt most weak and frightened) in the arms of the lord.

2

As the days passed, and Christmas drew steadily nearer, the building on Cutt Street and most of its inhabitants took on an increasingly festive air. The season had always been celebrated seriously at Hughes & Hughes. Downstairs, paper-chains and holly and magic lanterns began to sprout among the offices. And every department had its Christmas party, on succeeding days, each one graced for twenty minutes or so by the presence of Mr Hughes himself, who took the opportunity to thank everyone for their efforts during the preceding year and to hand out the envelopes containing the traditional Christmas bonuses. On the sixth floor too the season was decently honoured. Christmas cards began to appear in the post, sent by our friends who worked downstairs, or from people who had worked at Hughes & Hughes once and had moved on – 'Love and smooches from Angie in Streatham. Remember after the ice rink, Bri?' Frank made a sort of frieze out of red raffia paper and stuck it to the wall above his desk, and he and Brian would staple the cards to it as they came in. It made for a welcome flare of colour in that dark end of the room.

One morning the internal post brought us a card that from its jagged, torn edges and the smudgy crayoned

96

drawing that sprawled across its face was obviously hand-made. On close inspection, the drawing proved to be a highly obscene version of the Nativity. Though the sender had not chosen to sign his name, there was no doubt who it was from. Frank wanted to chuck it straight into the waste-paper, but Brian took it from his hand, smoothed it out, and then stapled it on to the raffia frieze with all the rest.

'It's Kenny's way of saying Merry Christmas,' he argued when Frank tried to object. 'Even if he doesn't know it.'

On the lower floors the fun and frolic gathered pace. Mistletoe appeared, and often now you would turn a corner and run into a couple locked in a passionate, damp embrace underneath a sprig of the stuff. Some people carried their own mistletoe around with them, and there were lively chases up and down the corridors. In all this, Hoover was very much to the fore, and often I would see her hurrying along on her high heels, her cheeks aflame with excitement, running down some nervous prey. She caught me once on the third floor landing, and after a moment's hesitation – for I was still, after all, the Ghost – advanced on me, lips puckered and arms outstretched. But the door to the Gents was just behind me, and I was able to step back into safety. It was her season. She was the spirit of Christmas at Hughes & Hughes and if I had thought, like Kenny, to manufacture my own card, I think it would have shown Hoover – Hoover rampant, stuffed full of lust and innocence and goodwill to all men.

So I was greatly surprised to enter the warehouse one morning, the Friday before Christmas Day, to find Hoover in a terrible state. She was crying and gulping, and shaking her head, and crying again. Brian had his arm around her trembling shoulders, and was trying to soothe her. Over at the desk, Frank had his head well down, was keeping out of it. I could see the boys not far away, looking puzzled. They were trying to keep on with their counting, but it was hard for them not to look up every few seconds to see what was going on, for Hoover's sobs were really heart-rending. As Christmas had spread its kindly light over our building, Hoover had seemed to look like a young girl again – or at least, looked no more than thirty – whenever I spotted her rampaging joyously from floor to floor. But she looked like a frail old lady now as she clung to Brian. Something had happened, something awful had happened to her. I slipped between two nearby tiers, and crouched down and wondered and watched.

Gradually Brian managed to calm her down.

'It's gonna be all right,' I heard him saying. 'Trust me . . . You do trust me, don't you, Cyn?'

She looked up at him through watery eyes and nodded.

'Well, then, if I say it's gonna be all right, that's what it's gonna be. OK?'

And after many repetitions of this kind of encouragement, she seemed at last to respond. At least she was no longer crying. When he smiled at her and teased her gently, she even smiled back. All the time Brian was gazing steadily into her eyes, and I could see she was drawing strength from him as if from a deep pure well. Nothing he said to her was the least bit memorable or original, but it did the job. Cheered her up and put her back on her feet again. At last she was able to leave.

'It always looks worse than it is,' Brian reminded her, as he eased her towards the door. 'Isn't that right, Cyn?'

'That's right, Bri,' sighed Hoover. 'It's very true.'

'OK, then. You remember that. And I'll see you round lunch-time. We'll have a few drinks, we'll have a laugh. OK?'

We heard her high heels going down the stairs, not

clicking in her usual brisk way, but not going like a funeral guest either. Brian waved to her from the door, then turned back into the warehouse. The boys got to their feet. They came towards him as he stood there, shaking his head.

'Poor old girl . . .'

'What's up with her?' John asked.

Brian looked up. Stared at them for a moment. I crept closer to hear.

'Her daughter's done a bunk.'

'From where?'

'Borstal. She took off. She's out there . . .' He gestured towards the loading bay, the wicked city, the whole wicked country beyond. 'God knows where she is.'

A pause. Then: 'Is she going to be all right?' Lawrence asked nervously.

Brian stared at him.

'How the hell should I know?' He looked away then, and in a quieter tone: 'I wouldn't bet on it.'

He rubbed his eyes. I guessed it had taken quite an effort from him to get Hoover's sorrow under control. Particularly when he felt she had every reason to be upset. Gloomily he looked over at Frank. Frank shook his head, very sober, obviously not hopeful either. Brian heaved a great sigh.

'Ah, Christ,' he said. 'Life's sad.'

Silence. The chilly air was thick with melancholy and foreboding. The boys looked at each other dolefully. I looked at the tin box in front of me. I wanted to be with the rest of them, to be thinking exclusively of poor Hoover and her troubles, and Hoover's daughter and the dangers she might be facing. But I couldn't keep my mind on all that. What I was thinking was that I had spent two years dusting this box and its several thousand fellows. For the first time, it occurred to me that it might all have been an outrageous waste of my life.

3

Altogether it seemed at this point as if we had a depressing morning ahead of us. But then Brian, in the way he had, seemed to shake himself, and in the same motion shake away too whatever might be bothering him.

'Ah, what the hell.' He straightened up, he stretched out his arms in front of him, and then to the sides. He smiled at the boys. 'It hasn't happened yet. Maybe it won't. Never say die, eh?'

The sudden change of mood caught the boys off-balance. Brian had his Senior Service out and was offering them round. Still somewhat preoccupied, the boys helped themselves. Brian now was completely back on form and, catching his mood, I picked up my feather duster and thought quite contentedly about getting down to work. It sometimes looked like heartlessness when Brian unloaded his troubles so fast like this, but I preferred to think he was like a fine general who wills himself to keep his mind clear and not go fretting over problems he can't immediately be dealing with. It also encouraged the troops, of course, to see him pressing bravely on.

'So,' Brian called out chattily, 'what are you boys doing this weekend?'

John and Lawrence looked at each other bleakly.

'Homework,' said John.

'In the holidays?'

The boys nodded glumly.

'Must be a funny sort of school,' Brian mused.

'It's like hell,' said Lawrence sincerely. He was evidently about to illustrate this description, when Frank got to his feet. Solemnly, and employing several bold though clumsy gestures, he addressed the others at some length. When he was done, he turned and lumbered off towards the door. On his exit, the boys looked at Brian for a translation.

'Haven't a clue,' Brian grinned.

They chuckled together, but there was no malice in it really.

'Ah, mustn't laugh, poor old sod,' Brian sighed. 'It's his teeth. They're getting looser all the time.'

Another giggle from John.

'D'you know what Kenny told me last year? Said that Frank was Mr Hughes' brother!'

Brian nodded. The boys stared at him.

'It's not true?' John said.

Brian shrugged. 'Hughes *and* Hughes,' he said significantly.

The boys now looked where Frank had gone.

'God,' said John blankly. 'How awful.'

I could see that Lawrence was much moved. Brian chuckled.

'He ain't a brother,' he said. 'He's Hughes' cousin.'

'Still – that's terrible,' Lawrence said.

'Now then,' said Brian sharply. 'It's not the end of the world up here.'

'All the same,' said Lawrence, 'you'd think they could do a bit better for him.'

'He's perfectly happy,' Brian said. He studied the still-shocked faces of the boys. 'What do you think

Frank's life's like when he's not here? After work, all he does, every night, he goes home, cooks himself a bit of rubbish, then sits down and watches TV till he falls asleep ... Well –' Brian thought for a moment, then conceded: 'All right, he's like everybody else, I suppose. But *still*, if he didn't have his job up here, it'd be bloody miserable for him. And he's not up to anything much better. And at any rate,' Brian added, with a rather cruel grin, '*he* won't be doing homework this weekend.'

The two boys grimaced. Brian glanced at his watch.

'All right, lads, you been up here half an hour since lunch. Job won't get done by itself.'

Obediently, they trailed off back to their boxes. In the absence of the invoices, Brian was at a loose end. He followed the boys over to where they were now working, side by side, at the tier next to mine. He hoisted himself up on to an empty shelf, and sat there watching them for a while. Then he took out a little pair of scissors and began clipping his nails, making sure that none of the debris would fall into the boxes.

Lawrence finished counting a box and put it back on the shelf. He glanced up at Brian.

'What are you going to be doing this weekend, Bri?'

'Me?'

Brian meticulously finished off a thumbnail. Held it out to admire it.

'Might go to the club.'

'With the schoolgirl?'

John's voice was rather muffled, and after he'd said the words he looked as if he wished deeply that he hadn't.

Brian stared down at him.

'I see,' he said coldly at last.

John looked up, shrugged unhappily.

'Kenny told us,' he said.

'Did he?'

John got hastily back to his counting. There was a tense ominous silence. But in the end, Brian only said:

'Yeah. Yeah, I might take her.'

John nodded, relieved to have got off so lightly. The boys worked on in silence for a little while. Then Lawrence straightened up, looked up at Brian. He was clearly nervous, but his chin was up and his mouth firm. He was going to say what he had to.

'Don't you think that's dangerous?'

Brian watched him, but said nothing.

'I mean . . . a schoolgirl.'

Still Brian watched him.

'Kenny said she was only fourteen.'

Suddenly Brian dropped to the floor.

'I did ask for your opinion?' he snapped.

He stood a foot away from Lawrence, staring him down. Soon Lawrence had to look away. Brian turned then and stalked off into the gangway. The two boys looked at each other. Lawrence rolled his eyes. John shook his head in warning. Lawrence stooped down once more. They both got back to their counting. It occurred to me that these comments about Brian's private life, which I had thought were just a bit of cheek, were in fact made out of concern. And friendship. I saw that they might have been taking Kenny and his threats seriously. Probably, I saw now, they had talked things over away from the warehouse, and had decided to find an opportunity to bring the matter up and warn Brian. I thought this was touching, their concern. I wanted to explain to them, however, that they had no need to worry: Kenny, for all his threats, schemes and nasty plots, had never yet been known to bring one of them off in real life.

4

I could see Brian standing in the gangway. He was looking back at the boys' bowed heads. He seemed for once not to know what he wanted to do. He looked surly and disaffected. His underlip jutted out. It appeared thick and uncertain, seemed to quiver in a vulnerable way. As he stood there, wavering, he rather resembled one of those victim-heroes of the previous decade, of my own teenage years, like James Dean or . . . well, James Dean. 'Mixed up', they used to call those characters. That is how Brian appeared as he stared back at the boys. He looked mixed up.

At last he shrugged, and made his way back towards them.

'Look,' he said quietly.

They sprang to attention. Watched him. He hesitated. Then:

'She's fifteen. She was fourteen, but she's fifteen now –' Brian stopped. Then, sighed and nodded: 'And she's a schoolgirl. But she's a *big* girl, y'know? And I didn't know how old she was when I met her.'

It was quite painful to hear Brian yielding up these explanations. The boys had grown self-conscious.

'Look, it's all right, Bri –' John started.

'*We* don't care,' Lawrence chipped in.

Brian motioned for silence. He got it instantly, of course.

'And it's not like I make a habit of it. All my other birds – well –' He stopped, rubbed his forehead. 'All right,' he admitted, 'I have been looking at younger ones lately. Don't know what it is. Maybe I'm turnin' into a dirty old man – but there's somethin' about a young bird, y'know? Funny little ways they got – and the skin, right? I like to touch their skin. And then they got a sort of smell . . .'

Brian seemed to fall into a reverie. The boys glanced at each other. They looked well out of their depth.

'Ah, well,' said John, after a pause. He smiled at Brian uncertainly.

And: '*We* understand,' from Lawrence, though it was clear to me he didn't.

Brian looked up, and smiled. 'OK,' he said softly, 'I just wanted to put you straight.'

They responded gladly to his smile. And to the way the uncertainty had dropped away from him now he had got his side of the story out into the open.

'You ought to meet my Dot,' he said.

'Dot?'

'Dot. Dorothy. You should meet her. She's all right.' He grinned suddenly. 'Even though she is a schoolgirl.'

Gurgles of understanding laughter from the boys. Lawrence, pleased that it had all turned into fun, pointed at John.

'He goes out with a schoolgirl too.'

'Well, I should hope so.' Brian turned to John. 'Gotta girl-friend, have you, Johnny?'

Embarrassed, proud, John acknowledged it was so. Brian reached into his pocket for his cigarettes. But

Lawrence beat him to it, producing a ten-packet of Nelson. Brian accepted one. He pinched off the filter tip with his finger and thumb and stuck the rest in his mouth.

'Is she nice?' he asked.

He held a match to John's cigarette, then Lawrence's. Then he blew it out. He struck another match to light his own. It was one of his old English superstitions. Third man on the match = unlucky.

John shrugged, and ducked his head.

'She's very nice,' Lawrence said, grinning at his friend.

'How's it going then?' Brian asked.

John hesitated.

'All right,' he said then, in a somewhat subdued voice.

'Trouble?'

John shook his head.

'No, not really. It's –' He sighed, defeated. 'It's just a bit difficult. We can't – you know – can't find anywhere to go.'

Brian knew straight away what he meant.

'What's wrong with your house?'

'My mother's always around.'

'Same with her place?'

John nodded.

'It's difficult, innit?' Brian said. 'I remember – before I got my own place – big problem that was. I used to take 'em up the park. But it's too cold for that now. You'd both freeze to death, half your clothes off.'

Brian frowned as he considered the difficulty. Then his face cleared.

'Why don't you bring her up here?'

John stared at him.

'Those sacks are very comfortable,' Brian said.

John swallowed. 'Do you mean it?'

'It's been done before. Lots of times. In the old days,' Brian added sentimentally, 'Hoover used to be up here all the time. Yeah, bring her in. You can borrow Frank's stove. It'll be comfortable. Private. She'll love it.'

While John thought the offer over, Lawrence stirred, opened his mouth to speak, hesitated, then asked:

'Why's she called "Hoover"?'

Brian gave him one brief, searching glance. Then shook his head, said:

'Use your imagination, Lawrence.'

'I'll do it,' John said. 'I'll ask her. You sure it'll be all right?'

''Course it will,' Brian smiled. 'What's her name?'

'Denise.'

'Denise. That's nice. We'll treat *Denise* like a princess. That's a promise.'

5

The three stood smiling at one another. I thought, watching them, that the arguments of the morning, then their reconciliation, followed now by this plan for John and his girl had all worked to bring them closer together. And I thought too that I was rather sorry not to be a part of this little circle. Sorry enough that I even tried to work out some way in which I could get myself included. Perhaps I could offer something – what? a blanket for John's girl? something else? But it was pointless, I knew. They had no need of me. And I had built the wall up around myself so high that if I climbed over it now it would appear as freakish to them as my staying behind it did. I had turned myself too successfully into the Ghost. I couldn't walk among mortals again – and anyway I hardly knew whether I really wanted to.

It was just a whim, I decided, brought on by my mild envy at the sight of those three enjoying their companionship. I had forgotten for a moment how necessary it was for me to stay hidden. It was a foolish idea to leave my hiding-place, a notion as ephemeral as the tranquil harmony *they* were sharing was likely to be.

And indeed in a few moments it was all broken up by Frank's return. He was clutching in his hand a very slim sheaf of invoices. There couldn't have been more than half a dozen of them.

'Is that all there is?' Brian grunted.

Frank nodded.

'The whole morning's?'

Frank nodded. Brian moved towards the desk, shaking his head. He looked over his shoulder.

'Right, boys. Get on with it.'

The boys stooped again to their work. Brian reached the desk. Moodily, he collected a few paper bags.

'I dunno, Frank. I remember you used to bring sixty, seventy-five orders up of a morning.'

Frank mumbled something about it being Christmas.

'Even at Christmas, we used to get thirty, forty even.'

Brian moved then to the centre of the gangway. Took a deep breath.

'OK,' he said.

Frank picked up the first invoice. I shifted myself to where I could get a better view. Frank stared at length at the paper in his hand. The seconds ticked away. A minute passed. Brian waited.

Suddenly he flung his head back.

'"I-I-I'll beee-e-e",' he called to the shabby, splintered ceiling. And this time hit the high note to perfection: '"Ho-o-ome . . ."'

His voice trailed away into a despairing sigh. Frank turned the invoice the right way up, and stared at it from this point of view.

'"Three-quarter-inch gimp pins",' he called out at last. (I give it in translation.) '"Three dozen".'

Brian leaped to a high shelf. Began emptying a box.

'Yeah?'

'"One-inch countersunks, half a gross".'

Above me, Brian rose in the air like a great stag. It was

a leap I had never seen him attempt before. He cleared the space not only to the tier next to him, but to the one past that too. In one bound. I heard the boys burst into rapturous applause.

'Get back to your work,' Brian called out as, without pausing to recover from the magnificent jump, he started to fill a bag.

His voice was stern, but I knew him well enough – Lord, how well I knew him by now! – to recognise that the ovation had flattered and pleased him all the same.

6

Since the day of the air-gun incident, and of the scene in Mr Hughes' office which had turned out so disappointingly for him, Kenny had stayed well away from the warehouse. The obscene Christmas card was the only sign we'd had of his continuing existence. Life certainly went on in a more tranquil fashion in his absence. There were no vicious rows, or name-calling, or screaming matches. Nobody fired off guns or tried to make Frank jump out of his skin. More than once I heard Brian say what a piece of luck it was that Kenny seemed to have dropped down a deep hole. I wasn't sure if it was only in my imagination that I seemed to hear a slightly wistful note in his voice when he said this. For myself, I had to admit, as the largely peaceful days went by, that I rather missed the youth. His entrances on the sixth-floor scene, unsettling as they were, had had a bracing effect too. Without them, the atmosphere seemed to get a bit too still and stuffy as time went by.

I was pleased therefore to look up from my dusting one day (the Wednesday before Christmas), just after lunch, and see that Kenny was lurking in the doorway. He seemed, as he peered this way and that, to be trying to establish exactly who was inside the warehouse. We were, in fact, down in numbers that afternoon. Brian was away taking a parcel to Waterloo Station, and John had been out on a job most of the morning, I wasn't sure where. There was no reason that I knew of why Kenny should want to avoid John. It had to be Brian's absence that, once Kenny had assured himself of it, caused him to throw off his caution and advance perkily into the warehouse.

He moved past Frank who was sitting hunched over the desk. He'd been sitting in this exact position for so long that I'd decided he must have fallen asleep. But Kenny took no notice of this splendid opportunity to startle him. He kept going, heading straight for Lawrence who was counting at a tier not far from the loading bay.

I crept along the gangway and insinuated myself between two nearby tiers.

'Afternoon, Lawrence,' I heard Kenny say brightly.

Removing a box that was blocking my vision, I could see that a most uneasy look had come upon Lawrence's normally cheerful countenance as he turned to acknowledge the greeting. I knew he had not forgotten his last encounter with Kenny. When Brian, for good motives I am sure, had tried to laugh with him about it the other day, Lawrence had turned away without speaking or smiling. Of us all – except perhaps for Frank – he had been most sincerely grateful for Kenny's recent absence.

'Where's young John?' Kenny asked.

'Downstairs.'

'Left you to do all the work, has he?' Kenny shook his head in sympathy. His manner was amazingly cordial. I had never seen him be so pleasant.

He looked around him.

'I left something up here the other day. Thought I'd pick it up.'

Silently Lawrence pointed to a corner. The air-gun still lay there where Brian had kicked it.

'Ah,' Kenny nodded. 'Right.'

But he made no move to fetch it. Instead, he continued to stand and smile kindly at Lawrence. Then he glanced down at the boxes where the boy had been working.

'Want a hand?'

'Oh . . . oh, all right. Thanks.'

Kenny took hold of a box. He began counting the contents in haphazard, lightning-fast style.

'Twenty-eight,' he reported.

He beamed at Lawrence as the boy conscientiously wrote the figure down on his bit of paper.

'So how are you, Lawrence?'

'Oh – fine.'

'Eyes all right?'

Lawrence swallowed. Kenny sighed in gentle self-blame.

'I get a bit carried away.'

'It's all right. Honestly.'

'Sure?'

'Sure.'

Kenny whizzed through another box.

'Forty-nine . . . so – uh – so I guess you'll be glad to be going back to school soon, eh, Lawrence?'

'Right. Well. You know. Not till January.'

'And what are you studying there?' Kenny enquired.

'I'm doing A-levels.'

Kenny cocked his head.

'How d'you mean?'

Lawrence stared at him as if uncertain whether it was a joke. After a while he said:

'They're exams.'

Kenny seemed to recognise then that he had been demonstrating particular ignorance.

113

'I left school when I was thirteen,' he explained. 'I was ill. I never went back . . . Ulcers.'

Lawrence's eyes kindled with quick sympathy.

'Did they get better?'

'No,' said Kenny gravely. A far-away note drifted into his voice, redolent of suffering bravely borne. 'I can't eat most things. Can't drink. I shouldn't ever get excited. I try and explain that to Brian but . . .'

He shook his head.

'I'm sure Brian doesn't understand it's so bad,' Lawrence said earnestly.

I saw a spurt of fury rise up in Kenny's eyes. But he restrained himself.

'Think so?' he said dreamily. 'P'raps you're right, Lawrence. But with ulcers you always have to be worried about . . . some accident.'

Lawrence was looking most concerned by now. Kenny put on a brave smile and, with a noble little wave of his hand, dismissed the whole sad situation, so fraught with danger, etc. I was wondering what on earth he was up to. After a year and a half of Kenny, this was the first time I'd heard the ulcer story. I was certain it was nonsense. I could see he was trying to establish some mood or bond between himself and Lawrence. I couldn't yet guess why though.

Kenny reached down to pick up another box of steel washers from a lower shelf. He gave a little effortful grunt as he did it.

'Here, I'll do that,' Lawrence said quickly.

'Ta, Lawrence.'

Lawrence began counting washers. Kenny leaned one shoulder comfortably against the tier behind which I was crouching. I saw his right hand drop into his jacket pocket. He took out a little plastic bottle from which he extracted

114

a mauve tablet. Lawrence looked round in time to see him pop it in his mouth.

'Want one?' Kenny offered.

Lawrence inspected the bottle.

'What are they?'

'Make you feel good. Go on, have a couple.'

At length, Lawrence shook his head.

'I don't think I will actually.'

'Suit yourself,' Kenny said easily.

'Thanks anyway.'

'No problem.' Kenny popped another tablet in his mouth. He beamed at Lawrence. 'So have you enjoyed yourself up here?' he asked.

'Oh, yes.'

'Made you feel at home, did they?'

'Absolutely.'

'Good. They can be a bit funny, these blokes: Brian, poor old Frank –'

'I like them.'

'– but on the whole they're a good bunch.'

'That's what I think.'

'Yeah, I got a hell of a lot of respect for Brian,' confessed Kenny.

In my hiding place, I could hardly stop myself from laughing out loud at that. And even Lawrence, who found it hard to discover guile in another, raised his eyebrows suspiciously. Kenny grinned a little sheepishly.

'That surprise you?'

'Well . . .'

'Now I didn't say I thought he was perfect. For one thing, he's got a temper. You can't say he hasn't.'

Fair-mindedly, Lawrence nodded.

'But then,' Kenny argued, 'he's had a very sad life. He's

115

quite old, of course. Did you know he done National Service?'

Lawrence, back now to his counting, shook his head.

'Yeah. In the Navy. That's the famous club he goes to. All these old sailors and Teddy boys and rubbish like that. They sit around in this dump round the back of Tottenham Court Road and drink Scotch and go on about the good old days. Here!' Kenny sniggered. 'Some time, if he takes off his shirt, have a look. He's got two f——n' great crossed Union Jacks on his chest and underneath . . .' Kenny demonstrated on his own narrow torso. 'Says: "HMS Intrepid – England Expects". Sad, innit?'

Lawrence shrugged uneasily.

'Oh, well . . .'

'Sure. Right.' Kenny nodded quickly. 'Perfectly harmless, right. Although . . .' His eyes narrowed almost to slits as he watched the boy at work below him. 'I never really trust these old guys that have done National Service. Does somethin' to them. Know what I mean? They're sort of . . . *cautious*. Yeah? Bit stick-in-the-mud.' He leered hopefully then. 'Not like you and me, eh, Lawrence? Up to date! On the move! All that.'

Lawrence was giving him no encouragement. He had his head down, bowed over the boxes. I pressed closer against the shelves. I didn't want to miss anything. I felt Kenny had cleared the ground now, and was moving in on his target.

Kenny fed himself another pill. Took a deep breath. Forced up another ingenuous, sympathetic smile.

'So – Lawrence – what's your opinion of the unions?'

Lawrence looked up in surprise. I could see he wasn't certain he'd heard right. I knew he had though, and I knew too that Kenny's hitherto obscure goal had drifted at last into view.

116

'Sorry?' said Lawrence. 'Did you say –?'

'Unions,' Kenny nodded. He smiled disarmingly. 'Trade unions. What d'you think of 'em?'

Lawrence straightened up. I could see he was pleased at the turn the conversation had taken.

'I'm for them,' he said.

'Are you?'

'Definitely.'

'Good,' said Kenny. 'Only we're thinking of having one here.'

'Great. Fine. That's a really good idea.'

'Well, I think so,' Kenny nodded. ''Cause the money's not too good here. How much are you getting?'

'Seven pound ten.'

'Pathetic, innit? And we're not doin' much better.' Kenny moved into the gangway and called to Frank who seemed to be stirring at last. 'Oy. Frank. How much are they payin' you here?'

A roar of something that was possibly 'Mind your own business!' came from the far end of the warehouse. Kenny turned back with murder in his eyes, and a smile of gentle forbearance on his lips.

'Anyway it won't be much,' he said. 'And he's been here for ever.'

Lawrence shook his head, distressed.

'And me –' cried Kenny in quite genuine outrage. 'I'm gettin' less than ten. And I'm *skilled* . . . And I want to get married. I met the girl of my dreams,' he went on sentimentally, 'and we want to get hitched. How can you get hitched on less'n a tenner a week?'

'You can't,' said Lawrence decisively.

'Right. So . . . so we got up this sort of petition, you see.'

And Kenny drew from his pocket the grubby sheet

of paper that I'd last seen on the day Hoover had signed it.

'To get the union in here,' he explained. 'So they can sort things out. And I can get married. And poor old Frank can get a fair shake for once.'

Kenny looked down at the paper. And then, as if the thought had just occurred to him:

'Here. I don't know if you'd care to sign it? Everybody else has, more or less. I brought it up for Frank actually. But now that I'm here – and you're here –'

He got a biro out of his inner pocket, held it out to Lawrence.

Lawrence regarded the instrument doubtfully.

'D'you think I ought to?'

'What?'

'Well, I'm not permanent.'

'It's just another signature, you know,' Kenny observed mildly. 'Makes no difference to me, if you sign. It's just you said you was in favour of the unions and that. So I thought: well, here's your opportunity . . .'

'Right,' said Lawrence firmly. 'I am. In favour. OK.'

And he seized the pen and signed his name with a flourish.

7

Almost before the pen had stopped moving, Kenny had whipped the paper away from Lawrence.

'I done it,' he crowed. 'I done it!'

And as Lawrence stared in astonishment, Kenny danced into the gangway, waving the paper above his head. For once it only added to his pleasure that he should see, at that moment, Brian strolling in through the doorway.

'Go away, Kenny,' said Brian automatically. He threw the evening paper he was holding on to the desk.

But Kenny was not to be suppressed this time. He shook the sheet of paper at Brian and he twirled along the gangway.

'I got it,' he shouted. 'Twenty-seven! I got it.'

Brian came to a dead stop. He stared at Kenny. While he had been looking a little bit pleased to see that Kenny had shown up in the warehouse again, now his expression was very serious.

Kenny laughed wildly and waved the paper in Brian's face.

'Two-thirds of the f——n' work-force. I got it!'

Brian spun round to stare at Frank.

'You silly bugger,' he snapped.

'Wa'n't me,' Frank protested.

119

Puzzled, Brian turned back to Kenny. At that moment, Lawrence moved uncertainly into the gangway. Brian gazed at him. And then walked slowly towards the boy. Lawrence seemed to shrink a little as he approached.

'You stayin' on here, are you?' Brian enquired in a conversational tone. 'Packin' in school?'

Lawrence shook his head. Nearby Kenny was gloating over his sheet of paper.

'No,' said Brian. 'Thought not. Just doing us a favour before you go, is that it?'

Lawrence had nothing to say.

'Twenty-seven!' Kenny cried gleefully.

Brian turned to look at him.

'They won't count *him*,' he said, and I saw poor Lawrence wince as Brian jerked a contemptuous thumb in his direction. 'He's just temporary.'

'He's a f——n' employee. Why shouldn't they count him? I got it!' Kenny cheered yet again. 'Two-thirds. That's what Hughes said.'

Brian, cool in the heart of this crisis, watched as Kenny capered around him.

'How d'you know you got twenty-seven?' he asked.

Kenny stopped dancing. Stared at him.

'What?'

'You can't count. You're worse than Hughes.'

And Brian turned dismissively away. Kenny gazed after him. Then looked down, puzzled, at his paper. His lips moved as he counted. A scoffing grin rose to his lips when he'd finished.

''Course I got twenty-seven. Count 'em yourself if you want.'

He thrust the paper at Brian. Brian took it and with a few swift movements tore it into many small pieces. He showered them upon the floor.

'I only saw twenty-six,' he said, and stared into Kenny's disbelieving eyes.

'You c—t,' Kenny whispered after a long, terrible silence.

He dropped to his knees and began to scrabble frantically among the bits of paper.

'Oh, you *c—t*, Barstow!' he screamed, sounding almost demented.

Brian watched him. He looked very pale and his mouth was set tight and grim.

Lawrence stepped forward.

'I don't think that was right,' he stated.

Brian turned to stare at him. But Lawrence did not look away. He met Brian's eyes boldly.

'They need a union here,' he said.

Brian shook his head and looked away. But Lawrence was not to be thrown off.

'The money's not good here, is it?'

Brian swung back to him.

'The work's not very hard. Is it?'

He looked down at Kenny who was trying to piece together the bits of paper. It was a hopeless task. Brian watched him soberly for a moment or two. Looked up again at Lawrence, again shook his head.

'You get a union in here,' he said, 'they'll raise the wages. Company can't pay it. It's on its last bloody legs as it is. They'll be sacking people, right and left.' He pointed along the gangway at Frank. 'He'll be the first to go, even if he is a relative. Downstairs – there's a few old girls down there that can't do a stroke. Hoover, she'll be out . . . They'll all be out. Except –' He gestured at Kenny, who had given up trying to fit the scraps together and was sitting on the floor, rocking to and fro in his agony. '*He'll* be all right. He'll be running the union. They won't dare fire *him*.'

'They won't fire *anybody*,' Kenny raged. He pulled himself up on to his knees. 'The f——n' union won't let 'em.'

Brian snorted at this. 'Ah, Kenny . . .' he sighed. He looked almost as if he wanted above all to make Kenny understand. But the youth wasn't listening.

'It doesn't have to be like that. They could make this place pay. They could do things.'

'Like what?'

'*I* dunno . . .' Kenny raised his hands and waved them about, sketching great schemes of improvement in the air. 'They could put in a lift,' he came up with at last.

Brian laughed.

'They could do a lot of things. They could make it pay,' Kenny insisted. He had got to his feet by now. Was standing squarely in front of Brian. 'It doesn't have to be falling apart.'

'With Hughes in charge? Bollocks.'

'Why does it have to be Hughes?'

'It's a family firm, isn't it? So they're going to keep it in the family, aren't they?'

'So – he gotta have some relatives. Maybe one of them's got somethin' on the ball.'

Brian shook his head wearily.

'He must have *one* relative,' Kenny insisted in his desperation.

Brian looked up towards the desk.

'Over here, Frank,' he called. 'You're wanted.'

Frank looked up, puzzled.

'Wha'?'

Brian gave him a reassuring wave, looked back at Kenny.

'I tell you,' he stated, 'bring in a union here, they'll

have to close the place down. Six months. A year. No more. That what you want?'

Kenny struggled for a moment. Then:

'Yeah!' he bellowed. 'F——n' dump. Yeah. If it don't deserve to live, then f—k it, let it die!'

Brian regarded him for a little while. He nodded then.

'You're a nice boy, Kenny,' he said.

He turned to walk away. Kenny took a step after him. His face was livid with hate.

'You don't want a union here, you know why?'

Brian turned back, watched him. There was spittle around the corners of Kenny's mouth.

'You don't want any other f——r running this place. Aren't I right? You want it your way. You up here. Hughes down there. Like always. And f—k everybody else.' Kenny's voice had risen again to a scream. 'That's what you want. *Don't* you?'

A moment. Then Brian took a step towards Kenny. His fists were clenched tight.

'He's got ulcers!' Lawrence cried out.

Brian stopped, looked at Lawrence, perplexed. At that moment Kenny burst into tears. The others stared at him as he tried to hide his eyes. Even Brian looked discomfited now.

At last, Kenny smeared his hand across his eyes, looked up, his face contorted.

'I'll fix you, c—t,' he spat out.

Brian turned away again. Now he seemed sickened by the whole thing.

'I'll get them to sign again,' Kenny vowed. He pointed at Lawrence. 'He'll sign again . . . Won't you?'

Lawrence hesitated. He looked up to find Brian now watching him. Then he looked awkwardly towards Kenny.

'Perhaps I'd better think about it. Sorry, Kenny.'

For a moment, Kenny wavered on the spot, distracted. Then he rushed towards the door.

'I'll *fix you, Barstow*!' he screamed again at Brian as he went past him.

'Something for you there, Kenny,' Brian called after him.

Involuntarily, Kenny stopped, looked round. Brian was pointing at the copy of the *Evening News* that lay on Frank's desk.

'Situations Vacant,' he said.

Kenny shook his head wildly, rushed onwards to the door.

'I mean it, Kenny,' Brian shouted. 'After Christmas . . .'

8

The silence in the warehouse, when the last sounds of
Kenny's racing feet had died away, was alive, like a shriek.
Brian stood there, still pointing at the paper, not moving.
Lawrence had backed against the end of the tier and was
leaning on it, breathing fast. At the desk, Frank had his
head well down.

And I in my refuge, I was shaking badly. I had seen
fights before – I had seen so many fights between these
two before – but this was something . . . a level of anger,
hatred, that was not normal, that was perverted almost,
like passion gone wrong, and ugly so I could hardly bear
to think of it. I had always thought of these two and their
scrapping like a Tom and Jerry cartoon. Fearsome blows
were exchanged, but they always bounced back in the
end. I couldn't see any prospect of that in the moments
that followed Kenny's exit. This had been too much.
Unforgivable things had been said, had happened. There
was no way back.

Brian stirred at last. On his face was an expression of
great unease. He looked round at Lawrence. Stared at
him blankly. Then looked away.

'Get on with your work,' he muttered.

Lawrence dragged himself away from the tier. Went

slowly to the lower shelf where the box he'd been working on lay. Brian waited until the boy was settled down. He put his hand up then, rubbed his eyes and his mouth. He walked down to the desk.

'All right, Frank?'

Frank grunted. He didn't look up. I think he was too alarmed almost to move. Brian watched him for a moment, then turned away. He walked back to the centre of the gangway. He came to a stop where the bits of torn-up petition had landed. They lay there, ruffled from time to time by the faint breeze that came in through the loading bay. Brian crouched down on the floor. He picked up some of the pieces and tried to fit them together. But it was impossible. He threw them away. Stood up.

He walked over then to the phone. Picked it up and dialled two numbers. Listened.

'Is Kenny down there?' he said into the phone.

The answer was negative evidently. Brian nodded, replaced the receiver. He paced up and down the gangway for a while. Then came to a stop. Stood there, thinking, scowling. Suddenly he put his head back and shouted out:

'What do I care? I'm goin' on a *liner*.'

He stood for a moment longer, the echoes of his cry dying around him. Then he walked down to the tier where Lawrence was working. Lawrence looked up as he approached. They watched each other. Brian put his hand in his pocket and took out his Senior Service. He opened the packet, moved a couple of cigarettes up from their rank. Held out the packet to Lawrence.

Lawrence got slowly to his feet, and came and took the cigarette. Brian lit them both up. He took a great drag, and released the smoke in a long, exhausted sigh. He looked again at Lawrence, shrugged awkwardly.

126

'I could have done without that,' he said.

'Yes,' said Lawrence.

They grinned at each other faintly, and I felt the tension in the room at last begin to ease away.

'I'll sort it out with Kenny,' Brian promised. 'It went a bit far. I –' He brooded for a moment, picking some tobacco shreds from his underlip. 'I'll sort it out somehow.'

I heard footsteps again on the stairs. Brian looked around. Then hoping, I guessed, or fearing that Kenny had come back for a second round, he moved swiftly into the gangway. I saw his expression become surprised, curious as he looked towards the door. Not Kenny then, I knew. I crept closer to the gangway myself to see who it was.

In the doorway stood John. And just behind him, smiling demurely, was a young girl.

9

'We're here,' John said. 'Er – this is my friend Denise.'

'Hello,' said the girl. She stepped forward. 'I'm very pleased to meet you.'

On John's face was an expression of bashful pride. He had every reason to look this way, I thought. His friend was very attractive. She was about sixteen, small and dainty. She had a little heart-shaped face. Her hair was a fairish brown, cut close, a wispy cap over a head that appeared so fragile it touched your heart to look at it. I thought it was a great improvement on the hair-styles that every other girl seemed cursed with at this time – the grotesque lacquered 'beehives', and the new geometric designs. She was wearing a shiny plastic coat, very fashionable then. I don't recall the colour, only that it was bright and that it glistened even in the dim light of the warehouse. The front was open, and I could see that underneath she wore a grey dress of the type known as a 'sack'. This style, which was of no help to many figures, was perfect for her, just touching and outlining the delicate lines of her body.

I couldn't quite see her eyes at first – and those I always thought set the final tone on a face, reducing the total effect in many cases, raising it in a few. I shifted my position for a better sighting – and my movements caused her to glance suddenly in my direction. I had an excellent view therefore of what I was looking for – and indeed it *was* excellent. A pair of bright green eyes staring at me. They were slightly slanted, like a cat's, and they gave to her demure and girlish expression a provocative sparkle of adult mischief. Then she looked away from me, and she was again the shy and artless schoolgirl.

It was all lightness, freshness, daintiness – yet, oddly, when I look back my lasting impression of Denise is of quite a solid little customer. For one thing, she had a habit of looking very directly at people from those sloping green eyes. She was looking now directly at Frank who, gripping the table-top in his big hands, had pulled himself gallantly to his feet. She looked at Brian then who stood, poised, halfway down the gangway, staring at her. Perhaps she felt in the air a residue of this afternoon's troubles, for a look of concern passed over her pretty face.

'Are you sure it's convenient?' she said.

Brian proved himself then to be a perfect host. I think he was very pleased at the turn events had taken. Even with his ability to shrug off his cares, he would have found it difficult to forget soon what had happened between him and Kenny. But this – this changed everything. The very air seemed to be changing now with the arrival of Denise, as if this bad winter's day had bounded suddenly forward into spring.

'Convenient?' he cried as he advanced upon the young couple. 'We were all wondering where you'd got to.'

He took the girl's hand and, holding it, smiled down at her.

'I'm Brian. This is Frank. And over there . . .'

He waved at where Lawrence had emerged, grinning, into view.

129

'Hello, Lawrence,' she called.

''Course you'd know him,' Brian chuckled. 'Old pals, eh?'

He noticed then that he was still holding her hand. Gently, he dropped it. He looked around. 'Right,' he said. 'Let's sort things out.'

'It's very kind of you,' Denise said. 'Is it really all right?'

'Promise you. I'm delighted. Frank's delighted. Aren't you, Frank?'

'Aaaargh.'

'And he's going to lend you his stove. OK, Frank?'

Brian picked up the paraffin stove and led the young couple over to the sacks.

'Now you'll be perfectly private here. We'll be over there –' Brian pointed to the desk. 'Long way off. And by the door so nobody can come in out of the blue. These are really comfortable,' he added, bending over to pat the top layer of sacks. He frowned at the little clouds that puffed out from under his hand. 'Didn't realise it was so dusty here.'

'It's all right, Brian, we've brought some sheets,' John said, and he touched the shopping bag he was carrying.

'Right you are,' Brian nodded. 'Well, that's it . . . How about a cup of tea?'

The young people looked at each other.

'Well,' said John shyly. 'Perhaps a bit later.'

'Of course.' Brian looked the pair over speculatively. 'Half an hour be all right?'

They thought it would.

'Sugar?'

'One lump, please,' the girl said.

'One lump,' repeated Brian, charmed. 'Milk?'

When he had taken their orders, he removed himself

130

with perfect tact. I saw it had been an insult to him that I had been praying that he would not hang around leering as the young couple made up their temporary bed. Or worse, that he would crudely wish them 'good luck' before he went. Nothing of the kind. He said not a word to them, did not even smile, just left.

He got hold then of Lawrence who was hanging around in the gangway not far from the space where the sacks were. There was a trace of sourness on Lawrence's usually open and friendly countenance. I wondered if he was feeling some envy towards his friend. Having set eyes on Denise, I could not blame him if he was.

Perhaps Brian had guessed the same as I had, for he immediately gave the boy something to do.

'Go down and get the tea, Lawrence.'

'Right,' said Lawrence, and he did brighten up a bit to receive this commission.

Brian gave him a pound note.

'Get some cakes too. Buns. You know . . . Don't hurry. Come back in about forty minutes.'

When Lawrence had gone, Brian went to Frank's table and drew up a chair. The two men smiled at each other as he sat down. Frank reached up and turned on his little radio. It was tuned to Caroline. P.J. Proby came on bashing out his stuff. Brian then pulled a drawer open and got out a shabby box of cards. He dealt a couple to Frank, a couple to himself. Frank called for another. I was between two tiers now, parallel to the desk, and was quite near to the gangway. Suddenly Brian looked up from the cards and stared directly at me. I stared back at him. After several moments, his right eye closed in a slow, amused wink. And I found myself starting to grin.

Brian turned back to the game. Frank had thrown in

131

his hand. Brian slipped Frank's cards and his own to the bottom of the pack. He dealt out four more.

I pulled back, away from the gangway, receding again into darkness. I could still just see the two men, however. There was a quieter song on the radio now, and I could hear the slap of their cards on the table and their murmurs as they called their bids. If I listened very hard I could hear too certain distant sighs, sometimes urgent, sometimes gentle and drawn-out like a caress. And underneath this, I could hear too, a faint rhythmic sound as of tiny wet hands clapping together. Christ, I wanted to fuck somebody I thought suddenly, and so keenly that I pushed my groin hard up against the nearest tin box. And I realised then, as the feeling washed over me and slowly subsided, that I had felt nothing like this, nothing at all, for over two whole years. Seven hundred and forty-two days.

'Pontoon,' said Brian quietly, and he laid his cards out on the table.

IV

1

It was Christmas Eve. All over the building the last pretence that there was any work to do had been given up. And though people were due back on the 27th, it would not be adopted again in earnest until after New Year's Day. No typewriters clicked anywhere, nor telephones rang. The door to the mail-room was padlocked. Yet everybody had turned up, they had all 'come into work', for nobody wanted to give Christmas Eve on Cutt Street a miss.

Brian had spent grandly this year, and on the afternoon before the great day the ropes and pulleys at the loading bay had winched up to the sixth floor several crates of beer and a case of spirits. A sufficiency of paper plates and cups had been added to the store. Today the boys had been given a tenner and sent out with orders to bring back a supply of crisps and mince pies, sausage rolls, pineapple chunks, funny hats and Christmas crackers. You could – as after a certain age one can't help saying – buy a lot for ten pounds in those days, and when the boys came back with their loot they piled up on Frank's desk what looked enough to feed and entertain a small army. It was needed. All day long little deputations from the offices below, or from neighbouring buildings along Cutt and

135

adjoining streets, climbed the stairs to the warehouse. As each small celebration overlapped, the party grew and grew. The crowd spread away from Frank's desk to fill the gangway and spill over between the tiers. John and Lawrence had been deputised as waiters, and they moved, smiling and efficient, among the guests with trays of drinks and snacks. Brian stood near the desk, warming his backside against Frank's stove, smoking a big cigar, and welcoming each new arrival.

In one corner they were muzzily singing carols, in another they were telling jokes, each raconteur managing to cut off the punch-line of the previous gag in his anxiety to get in with a new one. It didn't matter – the laughter over there was constant and uproarious. A couple was embracing on the sacks. It was the same couple that had embraced there last year, and the year before. Their passion was awesome to behold. The rest of the year I think they hardly exchanged ten words. There were more frolics near the desk. It was the tradition for the women of Hughes & Hughes, on this single day, to flirt with Frank, hug him and tease him, bestow upon his big unhandsome face their fondest, wettest kisses. It came as a great surprise to him each year, but – because he could tell there was no cruelty in the fun – it was always a pleasant surprise. It was a treat to see him sitting there, grinning shyly, waving his great hands ineffectually about to ward off the amorous women as, squealing, they smothered him against their bosoms, and pressed their lips to his. He never touched them, or kissed them back. I don't know if it would have spoiled the game if he had. It just seemed to be the rule.

2

By mid-afternoon the party on the sixth floor was running down at last. The couple on the sacks finished their business and departed. As in previous years, for all the huffing and puffing, it had been a pretty chaste encounter really, the clothing on either side only disarrayed, not removed. One old boy from the mail-room, who on his entrance had more or less commandeered a whole quart of whisky, had to be lifted downstairs. There had been some discussion about whether he could be sent down to the ground via the loading bay, but Brian put a stop to such reckless talk. Everybody else went off in a reasonably orderly fashion. We could hear them singing on their way, the voices growing fainter as they descended to each successive landing.

It was, we agreed, when we were finally alone, one of the better parties the sixth floor had thrown. Of course, my memories of these events went back only a couple of years, but Brian and Frank could look down through the decades, and in this perspective too today's affair had measured up. Nobody had vomited, or pissed themselves, there were no fights, the spirit of Christmas had been with us today, we felt. Brian turned up the radio above Frank's desk as we moved about, clearing up the debris that had been left behind. I held open one of the sacks – when I'd picked it up, it had still borne the impress of the love-makers – and John and Lawrence shovelled tinsel and bottles and half-eaten mince-pies inside it. The hit-songs of that Christmas week drifted around us as we worked. The Beatles. The Rolling Stones: 'If you see my Little Red Rooster/Ple-e-eze drive him home.' Val Doonican and 'Walk Tall', Petula Clark and 'Downtown', the Bachelors and 'No Arms Could Ever Hold You'. And, of course – three times by my counting, as we listened – Elvis with 'Blue Christmas'.

A great party. And only two absentees from it. (For even Hoover, though still quiet and depressed over her daughter's continuing disappearance, had turned up for a little while, and had accepted a drink, then another one, then found herself unable to resist joining in and then leading the amorous harassment of Frank.) The missing ones comprised Mr Hughes – though he was still confidently expected, for we were the only department that he had not yet visited this Christmas – and Kenny, who was not expected at all. Since the great fight, he had not been seen on the sixth floor. However, in the couple of days that had intervened between that horrible brawl and this joyous afternoon, he had been quite visible in the building. I had seen him on several occasions, moving about, now on one floor, then on another. I saw too that he had a piece of paper always with him, and I guessed he was trying to resuscitate his petition. With some success, it seemed. Even as I watched, several people wrote upon the paper. (And a little later I heard a rumour that once again only one signature was needed to make up the number that would force a union on Mr Hughes.) I had an idea that – though much disguised by the general good-humoured Christmas bustle – there was something in the air, a feeling of rancour, and of impatience. And it was directed at

Brian, and caused by his high-handed action over the first petition. The day before Christmas Eve, I actually heard somebody in Accounts say that it was a damn cheek what that fellow on the sixth floor had done. Then he saw me, and slammed shut the door, and I heard no more.

Whether Brian was aware of this surge of feeling against him, and whether – if he was aware – he cared a damn about it, I did not know. In any case, by now, three-thirty in the afternoon, day before the Big Day, I had forgotten myself about all these troubling undercurrents. Certainly no hostility towards Brian had been evidenced by any of our guests. They had been only too happy to shake his hand or kiss his cheek, according to sex, and to guzzle his booze. And here we were, now they had all gone, and the mess they had left behind mostly cleared up, gathering again around our leader, as he sat on the desk, swinging one leg casually back and forth, and finishing his fine cigar.

I don't know how we got around to it, but the boys were entertaining us by singing a few verses of their school song. This was a rousing piece, in whose lyrics God Almighty and rugby football were closely intertwined. A few words of Latin were scattered about too. The boys – part of whose 'clearing up', I had noticed, involved swallowing the dregs from each paper cup they'd collected – threw themselves into their rendition with near-manic gusto. At the end, they booed and brayed their contempt for what they'd been singing, and Lawrence fell off the box he was sitting on. As he picked himself up again, Brian was shaking his head in gentle wonder.

'Unbelievable. "Jesus is our captain St Paul is our scrum-half"? You're making that up.'

'I swear!' swore John. 'It's a crazy place.'

'Bloody madhouse!' blared young Lawrence.

'Mad! I bet your school –' John made a second attempt. 'Bet your school didn't have songs like that.'

The boys watched him. Brian was thinking it over.

'Did you have a school song?'

Brian shrugged easily.

'Can't remember,' he said.

The boys stared at him, clearly envious that his schooldays hung so lightly upon him. He took pity on their despair, used an attachment on his key chain to open a couple of brown bottles of ale, handed them over.

'Come on, lads. You'll be out of there soon enough.'

'Not before they mess us up totally,' John groaned.

'Right,' Lawrence seconded him with equal gloom.

'Come on,' Brian repeated. 'What are you going to do when you leave?'

'Get out of England!' cried Lawrence.

'Go round the world!' whooped John.

'Go to America!'

'Yeah!'

'Route 66 . . . Los Angeles . . . Tucson, Arizona.'

'Don't forget Winona.'

'Right!'

'Or maybe New Zealand.'

'Or Australia. That's only ten pounds.'

'New Zealand's free.'

'Australia's free too on the Big Brother thing.'

'True . . .'

There was a long pause. The boys, their smiles fading a little by now, pulled on their bottles of ale. When John spoke next, his tone had moderated considerably.

'Actually, I'm probably going into advertising.'

'So am I,' said Lawrence. 'Or television.'

Brian nodded. 'Sensible that. What d'you think, Frank?'

Glancing round he saw that Frank had produced a

bulging brown-paper bag from his coat. He opened the neck of this bag and showed it to us. Brian beamed.

'Ah, nuts!'

Lawrence looked foggily round him.

'Have we got any nut-crackers, Brian?'

'Don't need 'em. Just tell Frank what sort you want.'

'Ah . . . walnut please, Frank.'

Frank fished a walnut out of the bag. He rolled it between his thumb and forefinger and squeezed. There was a loud crack. The nut opened down the middle. He held out the two pieces to Lawrence.

'Brazil nut, please, Frank,' said John.

As Frank started on that one, Brian sipped his stout, looked around him in quiet content.

'Booze – nuts – smokes . . . what more could you ask for?'

As if on cue, from beyond the loading bay, came the strains of music. The inimitable holy blare of a Salvation Army band, refined and softened by distance. They were rendering 'Hark the Herald Angels Sing'. Brian reached over to turn Frank's radio off so he could hear the band better. He waved a concert conductor's hand at the noise. The boys got up and, a little unsteadily, went over to the loading bay and looked down at its source.

'"Joyful all ye nations rise,"' Brian began to sing, '"Ta-ta-ta-ta-ta-ta-tah/ With the herald angels sing/ Christ is born in Bethlehem/ Na-na-na-na-na –"'

He broke off for a swallow of beer. The boys wandered back to rejoin us.

'It's a wonder they still come around here,' John remarked as he took his seat.

Brian cocked an enquiring eyebrow.

'Don't you remember? Kenny pissed on them last year.'

Brian grimaced.

'Yes, he did.' He sipped beer thoughtfully. Looked over at Frank who was working on a cob nut. 'Wonder where Kenny is. He don't usually miss.'

I was wondering if it was possible that Brian was just unaware how disaffected, how *enraged* Kenny had been made. I had little time to examine this possibility though, for Frank was mumbling in a heated fashion and, as was his way, his passion made him more articulate rather than less.

'Good riddance,' was what he said.

'Yeah, maybe,' Brian nodded. 'Still – Christmas Eve . . .'

He looked a little depressed as he said that. Still, in his healthy way, he didn't let it sit on his shoulders. He threw it off right away, in fact. He grinned at the boys. 'Turkey tomorrow, lads!'

'Right!' cried John and Lawrence heartily, raising their bottles high.

'Christmas pud,' exulted Brian, sounding to me suddenly as if one of those joyously greedy cartoon characters that I used to love in the Christmas editions of *Radio Fun* and *Film Fun*, comics of my boyhood, had come to life and speech. 'Lashings of mince pies . . .' And then as suddenly as he had switched gears before, his smile dropped away, he sighed regretfully, pulled on his cigar. 'And yet you know,' he said, as the smoke drifted and billowed against the low ceiling, 'there's many poor sods that won't be so lucky tomorrow.'

The boys nodded, also suddenly solemn. Frank mumbled something. Brian gave him an ear.

'What's that, Frank?'

Frank repeated his rumble. Brian nodded gravely.

'Very true, Frank. Her for one.'

'Who's that?' Lawrence asked.

142

'Hoover's daughter.'

'Hasn't she been found yet?' John asked.

'No. No, she hasn't.' Brian brooded on the missing one's sad plight. He sighed at last.

'Well, wherever she is tonight . . . God bless the little lady!' He raised his bottle. 'Hoover's daughter!'

All of us followed suit with our drinks, and John and Lawrence intoned again, 'Hoover's daughter.'

So we drank to her – and I can't believe I was the only one to feel my sense of Christmas comfort and cheer measurably heightened by thoughts of the poor wretched girl out there somewhere in the gloom and damp and dark, lost, unhappy, perhaps in danger . . .

Not that one wished her the least harm, of course.

'Hey!' cried Brian unexpectedly.

We looked up – and then looked where he was looking. In the doorway now stood John's friend Denise. She smiled shyly under our gazes. It was so pleasing to look at her. On this winter afternoon, she was wearing black stockings, a black woolly hat on the back of her head, and a duffel coat, glorious flame-red in colour.

'Is it all right?' she hazarded.

'Come in!' Brian called, rising to his feet.

He cast a quick stern look at the boys, and they – who otherwise I fear would have remained lolling on their backsides like louts – jumped up. They made room for her between them. John and she exchanged hugs under Brian's benevolent eye. She settled down then, looked at Brian and smiled. He pointed at her bags.

'Been shopping?'

She smiled again and nodded. Brian, I could see, was entranced by her. He grinned at Frank.

'Isn't she lovely?'

Denise laughed. She was enjoying herself. I thought I

143

saw the merest hint of speculation in her teasing green eyes as she looked at Brian, and I wondered if perhaps John was fortunate that his stay at Hughes & Hughes would be ending soon. (Though not as soon, I had heard, as was originally intended; the inventory was still not yet finished, and the boys' employment was being extended into the week after Christmas.)

'I bet you've got a school song, haven't you?' Brian was teasing her now.

'Sorry?'

'The boys have been singing us their school song.'

'Oh, they would,' said Denise, sounding rather cross, I thought. John was looking sheepish.

'Go on,' Brian pushed her. 'What's yours? Bet it's a good 'un.'

Denise shrugged, then began chanting quickly: '"God be in my head/And in my understanding . . ."' She broke off. 'This is stupid.'

Brian chuckled. Passed over an opened bottle of light ale.

'It's nice . . .' He smiled at her until she looked away. 'So what are *you* going to do when you leave school – Denise?'

She looked back at him curiously, as if wondering – and yet really knowing – why he was questioning her so intently. She hesitated, then: 'I'm going to be a doctor.'

'There,' sighed Brian, in gentle wonder. 'Think of that, Frank. A *doctor*.'

And I didn't know whether I was imagining it, but in that moment, the moment after Brian had spoken of being a doctor – in this wondering way, as of something that represented an aspiration so far outside his own or his own kind's ken – I seemed to see shadows fall across Denise's pretty face. Of the iron bars of English class-consciousness.

For whereas a little before, as I have said, I thought I had seen her dealing with Brian speculatively, even flirtatiously – and there was no reason why she shouldn't: he was, as I must have made clear, a most attractive man – now she turned suddenly to John, and put her head against his shoulder. John, unsure quite how he had inspired this sudden show of devotion, put his arm around her, and smiled proudly, at no one in particular.

I should say that this sudden withdrawal by Denise put no strain at all upon our little gathering. Indeed, it was rather that our harmony – which might possibly have been threatened if Brian and Denise had gone on smiling and sparking at one another for much longer – was now restored to the perfection that had existed before her entrance. Here we were. And as Brian had said: what more could we want? Nuts, booze, smokes. Good friends to enjoy these with – and nobody presuming on this friendship to cross social or sexual barriers (well done, Brian: for I suddenly had no doubt that – not wanting to ruffle John and so spoil our Christmas tranquillity – it had been by design that he had reminded Denise of the gulf between them).

I looked around the circle. Each face was glowing with contentment. And I was a part of this circle.

I was a part of them.

The Salvation Army band, which for a while had been playing obscure, easily ignorable tunes, ascended into 'Silent Night'. The absurdly beautiful notes rose up through the loading bay. We on the sixth floor – except for Frank who was wrestling with an almond, and, intermittently, me who was watching the others – closed our eyes. It was an intense, a religious experience. We were in – I mean it literally – an ecstasy. All of us were.

145

3

Time passed. The scene on the sixth floor stayed much the same, except that everybody got even more relaxed and mellow, and that the band after their 'Silent Night' climax went away. Our revels were not left without musical accompaniment though as Frank's radio was switched back on. I remember 'My Boy Lollipop' by Millie was playing at one point. A little later, Brian was waving his cigar about and holding forth.

'You know, boys,' he was saying. 'You know, Denise, I went round the world with the Navy. Singapore . . . Rangoon . . . Suez Canal. There are some ruddy awful places in the world . . . And you know what? We grumble a lot, but – when all's said and done – we're very lucky really. Getting born here.'

He swigged his beer, looked kindly over the top of the bottle at John and Lawrence.

'Do you know that, boys? D'you know you're lucky? . . . John?'

'Sure, Brian.'

I could see John was being indulgent. He cast quick, amused glances at Lawrence and Denise. And they were returned in kind.

'How about you, Lawrence?'

146

'Sure, Brian.'

Brian had narrowed his eyes suspiciously at their too-ready response. I could see he had guessed he was being patronised, though he couldn't quite put his finger on the reason for it.

'You sure, Lawrence? I mean, you're a bit of a socialist, aren't you? Signing petitions and that . . . That right, Lawrence? You a socialist, are you?'

'Yes, I am,' Lawrence said stoutly. 'I don't know why you're not, frankly.'

'Nah,' said Brian, his easy temper returning as he spoke. 'Nah, I never vote. See, my whole philosophy of life is –'

He couldn't help himself then succumbing to a really enormous yawn. At the end of it, he masticated a few times, sounding, in fact, remarkably like an old man chewing on his gums. He seemed to have forgotten about his whole philosophy, though the boys and Denise were waiting eagerly to hear it. He looked over at Frank.

'Hughes should be up by now, shouldn't he?'

Not waiting for Frank's responding grunt, he looked back at the boys:

'Then we can all go home.'

Separately, we contemplated what that meant for each of us. I would be spending Christmas at my parents' in Uckfield. My brother Simon and his girl-friend would be there too, and assorted aunts and uncles and cousins were due to drop in over the holiday. I could contemplate all this without much fear. Over the past couple of years my family had been well trained in dealing with my behaviour. They would leave me alone, I knew. Completely alone, if I wanted it so. I could be as I was last Christmas, which I had spent entirely in my room. Meals appeared outside the door at regular intervals. Presents piled up out there

147

too as each successive wave of relatives broke against the house.

It *could* be like that again. But I was wondering now if that was exactly what I wanted this time. And I was remembering of last Christmas that, though thankful to have my sanctuary on the upper floor, it did get very boring in there by the second day, and even then – though I was much deeper in my darkness than I knew myself to be now – I was tempted to go downstairs, to the source of all the talk and laughter that I could hear in my room, and at least warm myself at the edge of the fun.

My musings were interrupted at that moment. Lawrence burst out: 'I'm going to be sorry to leave here.' And when Brian and Frank chuckled at him: 'I am. I'm going to miss it.'

'What's there to miss?' Brian said. He gestured round at the dim warehouse. Grinned as he looked back at Lawrence. 'Anyway – you're no good at the job. I had a look at those boxes . . .' He winked at Denise then. 'I'll have to do it all over again when they've gone.'

He nodded at John and Lawrence, who looked defensive, mutinous.

'That's terrible,' Denise declared indignantly.

'Don't listen to him, Denise,' said John. 'We did some checks on the boxes ourselves yesterday. We'd counted all right.'

'We've got a few more to do,' Lawrence chimed in, nodding at Denise. 'After Christmas, we'll finish 'em all. You won't have to do a thing, Brian.'

Brian held up his hands in mock-surrender.

'All right, boys. If you say so.' He winked again at Denise. 'It should be right. They've been at it ten days, the pair of 'em. I could do it in a day, easy.'

John nodded humbly. 'Actually, he could,' he told Denise. 'He's incredibly fast.'

Mumble of agreement from Lawrence.

'You should see him do the orders,' John added.

'What's that?' Denise asked.

'Oh, it's . . . *beautiful*!' Lawrence cried. Then blushed as we all laughed at him. 'It is,' he insisted, though not so loudly.

Denise looked back at Brian. I thought I could see that speculative look once more in her eyes.

'I wish I could see it,' she said.

'Do it for her, Brian,' John said.

'No!' cried Lawrence in outrage – and we all looked back at him. 'It's not a *performance*.'

John and Denise looked abashed. Brian stepped in, grinning easily.

'Ah, come on, Lawrence. Bit of fun.' He looked over at Denise. 'Would you really like to see it?'

His voice was low and warm. I could see Denise respond to it, in the way she smiled back at him.

And it seemed all at once as if Brian had forgotten about the little safety-barriers he'd erected between him and John's girl-friend. Probably due to the extra beer he'd taken on since then. Alarm bells started going off in my mind. But not too loud, for I had taken on additional ale too, and my thoughts were getting muzzier by the minute.

And anyway – what the hell. Let what would happen, happen. It was 1964 after all. Almost '65. The prison was opening up at last. People did what they liked now. With whoever they liked. It was freedom.

'I would,' murmured Denise. 'I'd love to see it, Brian.'

4

Brian slipped off the table. Removed his jacket and hung it up, carefully as always. He rolled back his sleeves.

'Come on, Frank,' he said.

He began sorting out some paper bags from among the party clutter on the desk. He found a couple, looked up. Frank was staring at him, puzzled.

'Read us off an order then.'

'We haven't got one (Han' go'un.)'

A moment. Then, in a gesture I remember as one of such infinite forbearance, Brian laid his hand on Frank's shoulder. Stood like that for a few moments. Then took his hand away, and opened a desk drawer. He got out a stub of pencil and a scrap of paper. Scribbled on it, gave it to Frank.

'Just shout that out, Frank.'

Like a bulb switching on in a dark room, the idea penetrated Frank's brain. He studied the bit of paper, licked his lips nervously. Then nodded. Brian positioned himself in the gangway. He winked at the boys, at Denise. They had got up off their boxes to watch him.

'Right, Frank!'

'"Quarter-inch steel hex",' droned Frank. '"Three dozen".'

Brian leaped for a shelf. A really sensational, chamois-like

150

bound. Cries of 'Oooh' and 'Aaaah' rose from the young people. Brian stuffed nails into his paper bag.

'Yeah?'

'"Half-inch King Dicks – one dozen".'

A huge leap on to the next tier, and then a lightning scramble over to the other side. There was no question Brian was showing off, taking risks he would not normally consider. Still it was fine to watch him. Beautiful, as Lawrence had said. Denise clapped her hands in her excitement. The kids moved along the gangway to keep Brian in sight as he placed two accurate handfuls into the bag. I saw he was sweating. I remembered suddenly how many bottles of beer he had put away this afternoon.

'Yeah?'

'"Two-and-a-half-inch japanned – thirty-two".'

The most sensational leap of all. High on to one tier, teetering on the top of it, and then without pausing to get a good foothold, casting off into the void to land on the next, which, as it happened, was set further apart from the previous tier than was normal.

We were all hurrying along the gangway to be in place to witness Brian's landing – when he disappeared. And next we heard a terrific bump and a cry of pain. We came to a stop. Looked at each other – more amazed that this could have happened to Brian than fearful, I think. Then, Lawrence calling out, 'Brian!' and John shouting, 'Are you all right?', we rushed to find our fallen hero.

But before we could reach him, Frank had reached us. And pushed past us. When we arrived in the space between the tiers, he was on the floor beside Brian, propping him up. Brian looked like hell. His left leg was stuck out stiff before him. He shook his head at our urgent questions – 'What happened?' 'Are you all right, Brian?' – not wanting to bother to answer them.

'Get me to a chair, Frank,' he muttered.

Frank scooped him up. We stepped back to allow them into the gangway. Carefully, Frank carried his burden to the chair by his desk. Carefully, he lowered Brian on to it. The young people had followed them. I was right behind them. In the light, I could see how pale Brian had grown. He looked up though and tried to grin at the kids.

'Are you OK?' John asked.

'Sure . . .' Brian shook his head, angry at himself. '*Stoopid*,' he said.

Lawrence turned to Denise.

'That's never happened before,' he said earnestly. 'I can't believe it's happened –'

'Shut up, Lawrence,' Brian snapped.

Frank was on his knees, asking Brian to move his leg. Brian screwed up his face in anticipatory pain. But the leg, after a creaking start, seemed to go back and forth quite fluently.

'Can I get you anything, Brian?' John asked.

'Bottle of beer.'

John obeyed. Brian flipped off the top, took a long swallow. Then looked at the kids, who were still staring at him anxiously.

'Come on!' he rasped. 'Have a drink. Christ's sake, it's Christmas.'

They wandered back to their drinks, smokes. They cast occasional glances at Brian who was sitting, brooding over his bottle, rubbing his leg from time to time. Frank had gone back to his desk, and was clearing up the party mess. I saw Denise whisper to John. I think she was asking him if it wasn't time for them to be going. I felt dreadful. It was all about to end; and end so abjectly. It would flavour the whole of Christmas for everybody.

5

'Hello! Hello! Hello!'

The deep, fatuous voice broke in on our gloom. We all looked over to the doorway to find its source. Mr Hughes stood there, beaming falsely. He was taking in the scene, and noting no doubt its surprising lack of zest. His big smile slipped a notch or two. Then he made a visible effort to get it back up again.

'Merry Christmas, everyone!'

Actually I think most of us were rather glad to see him. The events of the past ten minutes had been so unsettling. To see Brian, first in his glory, then tumbling like a rash fool to his ruin, and now hunkered down, in pain, surly, preoccupied – yes, unsettling. He just wasn't our Brian at the moment.

But Mr Hughes this late afternoon seemed entirely himself, and that was cheering. He advanced into the warehouse, still offering his extra wattage seasonal smile – though for connoisseurs of our employer's facial repertoire it was clearly only a shallow camouflage for his habitual mild and somewhat kicked-dog expression. He was carrying a large cigar in one hand, and as he looked at each of us in turn, he puffed on it grandly. He was just about to take another puff when he caught sight of

Denise, who had modestly removed herself to the back of our group. The surprise sent some smoke down the wrong way, and he had to pass through a fairly severe attack of coughing before he could find the voice to acknowledge her presence. And when the coughing was over, Brian cut in before he could speak.

'Young lady came down from Cosgrove's,' he said, referring to another export-import firm, situated in the alley adjoining Cutt Street. 'Wish us Merry Christmas.'

'How kind!' Mr Hughes beamed. 'And Merry Christmas to you, my dear.'

'Thank you,' said Denise.

'Excellent . . .' Mr Hughes nodded cordially to her, looked around at the rest of us. 'Well –' Pause for a puff on the cigar. 'Another Christmas.'

Nobody disputed it. He reached into his inside pocket and took out some brown envelopes.

'Here we are. Brian, Frank – I haven't forgotten the traditional . . .'

He watched as the two tore open the envelopes, began riffling through the contents, counting the bonus.

'And boys, a little bit more for you too . . .'

John and Lawrence came to take their envelopes. There was one more in Mr Hughes' hand. I saw him look down at it uncertainly. I stepped forward out of the shadows and stood before him. He looked up, saw me. Nodded, and handed the last envelope over.

'And thank you for *your* help too.'

Everybody had counted their cash now, had stowed away the envelopes. Mr Hughes' gaze fell on the table. There were still at least half a dozen full bottles of beer there, and a couple of spirits. I think he would have liked to have been asked what his pleasure was, and I saw Lawrence looking around at the others as

154

if he thought this was in order. I could have told him, it would never happen. As Brian had informed us at previous Christmas dos, the idea of handing out drinks and such to management gave him the creeps. (Though it was a fact that he was more flexible when the arrangement was the other way round.)

Mr Hughes sighed, but accepted the inevitable. He cranked up his buoyant smile again, regarded his troops.

'Another Christmas,' he announced yet again. 'Another year . . . And a good year for the company, you'll be glad to know. On the whole. Perhaps not as good a year as last year . . .'

His gaze at that point happened to fall on Brian. Who stared stonily back at him. And as if to avoid giving any hint that there had been some sort of personal accusation in his last words, Mr Hughes hurried onwards, tremendously fast:

'But I think we can all – I've said this in the other departments, I certainly want to say it here – we can all feel thoroughly proud of our efforts over the past twelve months. We can't relax, of course. We *daren't* relax. No. But I have no fears for the future. None. Because what we are selling here is not just nuts and bolts and . . .' (Here he waved his free hand vaguely at the shelves.) 'And *brackets*. We are selling the skill and knowledge and expertise built up from generations of experience. And *I* believe, in the long run, these qualities are bound to prevail. No matter –' His face darkened suddenly here, ominously. 'No matter how much shoddy, gimcrack rubbish is dumped on our traditional markets by the Ja-ja-ja-' He got it out finally: 'Japanese. Or anybody else. Whomsoever. I have *no* fears!'

Lawrence, young, enthusiastic, couldn't stop himself bursting into applause after this peroration. The clapping

155

was cut off very suddenly, and I guessed John had administered a swift kick to his friend. Mr Hughes, on whose face had appeared a hopeful gleam when the applause began, subsided into his usual self-deprecating manner when it ended so fast.

'Well – that's all,' he confessed. He looked hopefully round his audience. 'Now I want you all to come over the road for a drink. Brian? Boys?' Avuncular beam. 'Young lady?' And he even nodded invitingly at me.

Nobody spoke. And at last Mr Hughes got it. He turned to his cousin.

'And *Frank*. Of course.'

Everybody relaxed. Mr Hughes turned to go. Before he reached the doorway, he looked back over his shoulder.

'Try and make it before five o'clock,' Mr Hughes urged. 'I shall have to leave then.'

Nothing from Brian, though Mr Hughes' yearning gaze was imploring him to respond.

'Shall we say by five then?'

'Right you are,' Brian yielded graciously, as if wanting to put the poor old fool out of his misery. 'By five.'

6

John and Denise had somewhere they wanted to go, and Brian told them it would be all right to miss Mr Hughes' little party. They left in a cloud of 'Merry Christmases' and 'See you on Boxing Day' (from Lawrence). Their leave-taking was somewhat more muted than it might have been, for Brian was still absorbed in his wounded leg. He could hardly find the spirit to say a proper goodbye to Denise, for instance, just a 'Cheers then, love'. And she was not much more effusive. It was as if each rather regretted having encountered the other today. I guessed that Denise was feeling somewhat awkward and guilty about having flirted with Brian earlier. It hadn't helped that he had made himself ridiculous before her in his failed flight between the tiers. And had shown himself to her – as to all of us – to be so entirely mortal in his failure.

Still he also showed himself admirable then as we, the remnant, gathered closer around him, in that he didn't try to disguise his folly, nor the reason for it.

'I was showing off, Lawrence,' he muttered, still moving his leg back and forth. It was good to see his colour was so much better now. 'I was trying to look smart in front of that bint.'

'It was our fault,' urged Lawrence loyally. 'We made you do it.'

'I'm old enough to know better.'

'You did look great though. You really did. Until you –' Lawrence stopped.

'Went arse over tit? No, it was stoopid.' Brian shook his head. 'Me, half-cut, prancing around like that. Showing off.'

He put the foot of his bad leg to the floor. Stood up then, wincing.

'How is it?' Lawrence asked.

'All right . . . Ouch . . . Sprained me ankle, that's all. I'll be OK.' He sank back on to the chair. 'Soddit, I was going down Hammersmith dancing tonight.'

For some reason that struck Frank as very funny. He put his head back and roared. Brian watched him for a time, then glanced at Lawrence and winked. Then his gaze moved on to find me. And I think he was actually going to say something to me – when just then Frank's huge brays died away and in the silence we could hear footsteps on the stair.

I supposed – and I guess the others thought so too – that at this late hour on Christmas Eve, it could only be John coming back to pick up something he'd forgotten. But the figure that appeared in our doorway a moment later and stood there surveying our little group was definitely not that of our young friend. A middle-aged man, balding, fag between his lips. Wearing a light-hued raincoat over a business suit. Carrying a cheap-looking attaché case. He looked like the sort of man who came to our house to read the gas or electric meter. As if he was pretending to have a profession.

Into the suspicious silence we were offering him, he asked then:

158

'Does Brian Barstow work up here?'

A pause. Brian got to his feet again. Pain flickered at the corner of his mouth.

'Who wants to know?'

'I'm Detective-Sergeant Ames.'

A longer pause. Then:

'I'm Barstow.'

The policeman took out a large oblong wallet from the inner pocket of his jacket. From it he extracted a sheet of writing paper, heavily crumpled. He held it out. We could see the writing on it was done in a vividly green ink. I thought I recognised it. Light was dawning for Lawrence too, I saw.

'D'you know a young lady called Dorothy Short?'

'Kenny!' gasped Lawrence, involuntarily I was sure. Brian had time to glance at the boy curiously, then face the sergeant again.

'I know her,' he said.

'You'd better come over here then,' Sergeant Ames said, turning towards the tiers at the back of the warehouse.

'What for?'

'So we can have a little talk.' Ames was looking impatient. 'In private.'

A moment, then Brian shrugged and, limping quite heavily, followed the policeman into the recesses of the warehouse. We watched them go. Ames and his – what? prisoner? suspect? we didn't know – came to a stop. We could see them talking. And I sensed that, beside me, Lawrence's instinct was to go after them, to defend Brian. I think he would have used force to defend him, if need be. But there was nothing really to rouse him to the point of action. Only the low mutter of the policeman's voice. So he turned in frustration to Frank, shook his head angrily.

'Wha's goin' on?' Frank asked plaintively. I could see his honest, ugly face was full of consternation.

'It's Kenny,' Lawrence rasped.

'Ke'y wha'?'

'He's turned Brian in. Don't you remember? He said he'd fix Brian. The bastard!'

And Lawrence turned back to stare at the two men in the back of the warehouse, leaving Frank, I saw, even more confused and rattled than before.

In Lawrence's face I saw all the fears for Brian that I felt in myself. Arrest, disgrace, a trial, a term of imprisonment. What would be the charge? Corrupting the morals of a minor. Yes. No escaping it. I remembered very clearly the words of the letter that Kenny had read out to us. In honesty, I must confess that – together with images of young Denise, unclothed as I had never actually seen her – they had been the occasion for subsequent masturbatory activity on my part. (Another symptom of returning health, by the way.) I supposed that what had been left unread in the letter, the bulk of it, was at least as explicit, and therefore as damning to Brian's case.

I couldn't stand just to be waiting there as the inevitable unfolded before us, within our sight certainly, but out of our hearing to all useful purpose. So I drifted away into the tiers and made my way to where the two men were standing, close together, talking. Or rather, I saw as I crept closer, the policeman was doing the talking. Brian was listening, only nodding his head from time to time.

I advanced over one tier of shelves, down the other side, on to another. Not as Brian would, not spectacularly, but as befitting a ghost, slithering, silent, invisible. I had reached the tier behind which the two men were standing. Sergeant Ames' voice was still a little muffled. I put my hands on one of the boxes, and slid it, inch by inch, out

160

of its space. When it was free, I placed it carefully on the floor. Then straightened up to press my ear close to the open space. I could hear Ames clearly now.

'– all know about Dotty Short,' he was saying. 'Christ, half the blokes at the station have had her. Though not me, as it happens. But you're not going to find anybody who's gonna *blame* you, Brian. She's the sort you gotta beat off with a club. And like you say, she's a big girl. First time you meet her, you think eighteen at least. I understand that.'

Muffled grunt of appreciation from Brian.

'But the thing is – her dad. You didn't know about him?'

'I knew he was a copper,' Brian said.

'You didn't know he was DI?'

'Christ, I didn't.'

'OK,' said Ames, and I could imagine him nodding gravely. 'It's a delicate situation. If she ever started blabbing – and there's the proof right here.'

I heard a rustling. Could see the sheet of ring-book paper with the green writing on it opened before Brian's eyes. The colour was bright enough, I remember, to shine even in this gloom. I thought suddenly then of Denise's eyes – but before I could capture the thought, Ames was speaking again.

'Now I don't know who sent it to us. But I tell you frankly you'd have been spending Christmas in Brixton nick if it wasn't for . . .' Pause as if the sergeant was searching for the right words. 'The difficulty,' he tried at last. 'The awkwardness . . .'

'You think if I get done over Dorothy, it might come out what she's been doing with your blokes down the station?'

'As you say,' said Ames rather grudgingly. 'And she was even younger when she done it with them.'

161

Silence. Then another rustle of paper. I guessed the letter was back in Brian's possession by now.

'Take my advice, mate,' Ames said then. 'Be more discreet in future.'

'I am discreet,' Brian grunted.

'Then make sure your girl-friend is.'

'She's not my girl-friend. After tonight. Silly little twat –'

7

I crept away, not wanting to hear Brian in this vein, not thus descending to Kenny's level of sexual abuse. It was satisfactory that he had escaped the trap. Of course, I had expected no less. It was not for Brian to be caught in the toils that would have defeated a lesser champion. I was certainly pleased that my man, my contender, had proved himself again. That in spite of temporary setbacks – a nasty fall, a visit from the coppers – he had risen above fate and circumstances once again. And yet I was also entertaining another, quite contradictory emotion, as I made my way back towards Frank's desk. Back in the shelves I'd had a sudden vision of Brian being dragged away by two large, uniformed policemen, to face punishment for his disgraceful seduction of a young girl (albeit a big one, albeit a highly experienced one). And it was the oddest thing: as I'd contemplated this vision I had felt a stab of pleasure that was shockingly intense – and was taking some time to go away.

Of course, it couldn't happen. So far from dragging Brian away from us, Ames had a friendly hand on his shoulder as the two men strolled up the gangway towards the door. They stood talking for a little while in the doorway. Brian said something that made Ames laugh.

Then Brian turned, indicated the drinks, smokes, etc. still on offer on Frank's table. Would the sergeant care for . . .? The sergeant shook his head reluctantly. Of course, not while he's on duty. He shook hands with Brian. Waved to the rest of us who were standing gawping at the two of them like groundlings.

'Evenin', all!' Ames called in merry parody. 'Happy Christmas.'

Brian waited for a few moments until the clump of Ames' footwear had faded to a lower landing. Then he came back to us. He was holding the letter in his right hand. He got his lighter out from his jacket pocket. Flicked the flame under the paper. We watched as the green lines shrivelled and blackened. Brian flung it from him into the waste-paper bucket. It started a small fire, but Frank was there to put it out.

Meanwhile Lawrence had edged closer to Brian.

'Is it all right?' he murmured anxiously, and I remembered that, of course, he hadn't heard, as I had heard, how Brian had escaped his fate.

'Sure it's all right,' Brian smiled. And he actually reached out and ruffled Lawrence's hair. Lawrence looked honoured, as indeed he should.

'It was Kenny,' he said then angrily.

'"Course it was Kenny. Poor twerp.' Brian chuckled. 'I never told him what Dotty's father did.'

'What does he do?'

'Tell you later.' Brian winked at Lawrence as the boy stared in puzzlement. Then he switched his gaze a little to take in me – and I had the oddest sensation, as our eyes met, that he knew that I knew what had gone on. He grinned at me suddenly. For the second time this afternoon I realised that he was about to speak to me. And I – I backed away. Back into the gloom. Where I couldn't be talked to. Back

164

where I could see no one and none could see me. I wasn't ready yet.

I heard him say, but not to me:

'I'll have to sort Kenny out after Christmas, I suppose.'

He said this rather wearily, as of a chore to be undertaken, rather than something to be looked forward to. And then he said:

'And that's enough excitement for one day.' A pause. He must have been looking at his watch. 'Ten to five. Just time to get a free drink off Hughes. Come on, Lawrence. Let's go, Frank.'

In a few moments I heard the clatter of feet. They cleared the warehouse. Then, as I listened, descended the stairs. Silence now. I moved out of the darkness back into the gangway. I was alone.

I thought that – if I could have . . . if I only could have . . . I would be downstairs with them, over in the snug bar at the Lady of Kent, sharing a Christmas toast – maybe a joke – with Brian, or listening patiently to an anecdote from Frank, or explaining something to Lawrence . . . for instance, how not to end up like me.

I was so angry with myself. I sat on the chair by the desk, Frank's chair, and thought how much I wanted to be with them. I saw myself as split into two persons, the one desiring, the other forbidding. And I was bored rigid with the second one, who had held dominion over me for so long. And still held dominion. I could have – moments ago, I could have stepped forward into the welcome of Brian's smile. I could have just smiled back. Laughed with him at his close escape. For I knew, and he knew I knew. There was a bond. No need for explanations between friends. If I had stepped forward.

165

But the second person was still in charge, and I had stepped back.

I was about twenty minutes thinking of this, I suppose. I went through at least a couple more bottles of beer in that time. I hadn't been counting, but I was pretty sure I had drunk more this afternoon than I ever had in my life before, even at college. And yet, I was proud to note, I was still functioning, still thinking. I looked around me, at the cavernous empty room. The whole building felt like that to me suddenly, empty, vast. It had been dark now for some time. It was a setting, I thought muzzily, just right for a ghost. Christmas ghost.

But no, not me. Not me any more. If I could help it. If I only could. Yes, to hell with all that. To hell with the Ghost. To hell.

I drank to that. And then I drank some more. And in the end I don't think there was a single full bottle left standing. At least I couldn't see any.

I headed downstairs. Slowly. Carefully. Hand on the banister and one step at a time. On the third floor, I discovered that I wasn't after all the only person left in the building. Piece of luck for me, I thought – if one could dignify the delusions churning around in my head at that moment as 'thinking'. My chance to put my hand on the lever of history. What ghost could ever boast of that?

So I did. Put my hand. On the lever.

8

The inclination I had discovered in myself not to have a repetition of the solitary, tedious Christmases of the past two years was tested enough on this latest go-round. In fact, my Christmas turned out fairly tedious, but far from solitary. I made my intention clear on Christmas morning when I turned up in the living-room to share in the post-breakfast present-giving before the tree. Everyone – that is my parents, brother Simon and his girl-friend Sandra – was enormously discreet. Nobody commented on my attendance, eyes were kept tactfully down as I settled in my old place before the fire. Yet I saw the look of joy that passed between my mother and my father. It made me want to bolt upstairs, back to my room – but I held my place.

Tradition at our house required that the wrapped gifts were carried from the tree to each recipient – 'posted' – by the youngest person present. For all the years of my taking part that had meant me. But now I saw, even as I tried to steel myself into assuming my old duties, that my place had been usurped. I watched rather resentfully as Sandra got to her feet, and went to pick up the first present. I had an idea we were born in the same year. I tried hard to remember when her birthday fell. Mine was in February. Was it likely she had slipped in slyly with a Jan. nativity?

I tensed myself to make the challenge – and then all at once, like balm on my pain, the realisation rolled in that it didn't matter in the least. I need not challenge. I need not do anything. I could sit here like an adult, drink a little of the pre-lunch whisky my father was so anxious to pour me – no problem with that; I felt surprisingly free of hangover – and let the presents come to me. Let *Sandra* do it, for Christ's sake.

I think my presents were a success that year. Tie for Dad, tie for Simon, handkerchiefs for Sandra, a silk scarf for my mother. The ones I got given represented, I thought, a rather baffled goodwill on the part of the givers. Sandra gave me some railway insignia – badge, cuff-links – from the old London and Midland company. She must have searched high and low for these. I think Simon must have told her that I was interested in railway memorabilia, and so I was until about seven years ago. The brother himself gave me a long-playing record by the Dave Clark Five. I can't imagine why, it was a group I particularly disliked. From my mother and father came various sundry items in the tie-socks-hanky range, together with a cheque for a pretty fair sum.

The oddest gift, which was to turn out probably to be the most influential of any I ever got in my life, came from my mad(dish) Auntie May from Brighton. It was a copy of a fairly recent study of Victorian book design by one Ruari McLean. I have no idea what prompted this, for I had never expressed an interest in the subject to her or to any other member of my family. Indeed, I *had* no interest in it, as far as I was aware. And after tearing off the wrapping, and staring at the thing in amazement, I had laid it aside. I could only think that poor old May had been muddling around in the back rooms of some South Coast bookshop and had grabbed up the volume in a last-minute Christmas shopping panic. I remembered that in the early days of my withdrawal from human contact, my mother had tried to pass off my malady among her sisters by calling it an indication of my 'bookishness'. Perhaps that had started up some hare in Auntie May's intermittently fuddled brain.

Yet when, later in the day, the festive turmoil grew too great for me to deal with, when in fact – with the addition now of next-door neighbours, the Husseys, who had dropped in for a post-luncheon drink and had never left – my family was about to commence on charades, it was this little book I picked up on my flight from the living-room. And I do date my subsequent interest in books, and so, much later, the profession I was finally to enter, to that late Christmas-afternoon when I opened the pages of McLean's study. Read about the old printers. Whittingham and Pickering. Owen Jones. Joseph Cundall. William Morris, of course. And looked at the fine illustrations the old books carried, and the fine bindings that shielded them. I found it all quite fascinating. I don't know if McLean's work is still influential, or has been superseded. I have seen the title in one or two catalogues, and always mean to send for it, but never do. Actually, somewhat to my shame, I sold my own copy of *Victorian Book Design* some time in the late 1970s. Yet, as I say, its influence is always now with me.

The few hours I spent downstairs on Christmas Day, and a few more I threw in on Boxing Day in front of the television with the rest of the family, all that commonplace mingling left me feeling proud and hopeful and rather exhilarated. I went back to Hughes & Hughes the day after Boxing Day in excellent spirits (I think today's practice of treating the whole huge tract of time between Christmas Eve and New Year's Day as a holiday was not yet then so prevalent; it certainly did not operate at Hughes & Hughes). I found an atmosphere of almost funereal gloom on the sixth floor. Brian was sitting hunched over on a crate, staring at the floor. He did not look up as I, daringly, said hello. Only grunted. Frank muttered something, but also didn't look up, just kept on greasing his hands. I glanced questioningly at Lawrence who was nearby, and he nodded me towards the cork notice-board that was nailed up by the entrance. It usually carried only a two-year-old announcement of fixtures for the intra-office darts championships, or the photograph of a 'British Lovely' torn from *Tit-Bits*. But now I saw there was something new up there. A sheet of paper, brilliant white in the gloom, a short message typed upon it. I went to read this.

To All Departments [it said], As a petition to the effect has been handed to me today which carries twenty-seven names (i.e. two-thirds of the work-force), I am bound in respect of my previous undertakings to recognise the existence of a union at Hughes & Hughes. I gather that Mr Kenneth Glover, having been appointed pro-tem organiser for this union, will be in contact with all departments after the Christmas holiday. May I once again take the opportunity to wish every single employee a Most Prosperous New Year.

It was signed 'Malcolm Hughes'.

9

When I took up the duster for the first time that first day back I remember looking at it and hardly being able to identify it as a practical instrument of work. Rather it seemed to me like a folly, something ludicrous, something a medieval jester – a particularly desperate one – would wave around as he was trying to make the lord and his retainers laugh. I was assaulted once more by a sense of how greatly and for how long I had been wasting my time and my brain.

Yet habit very soon reasserted itself. In a little while I was back in the shelves dusting away. Not assiduously – I was never assiduous – but steadily enough. However, the atmosphere of gloom that I had resisted at first began to penetrate me too at last. Brian was the source of it, of course. As the days limped by, he was all the time horribly downcast and apathetic. There was no sign at all of his old energy and ebullience. He was not my hero any more. He sighed a lot. He frowned. He grunted when he was spoken to. He looked old. I saw Frank often looking at him worriedly. But he never tried to get Brian to speak of what was on his mind. Perhaps he was wise not to.

For we all knew what the trouble was. He was hurt, he was mortified. Everyone at Hughes & Hughes knew of his opposition to Kenny's proposals. And yet enough of his so-called friends had turned against him – had chosen *Kenny* above their loyalty to him – to get the thing started. A blizzard of paperwork emanating from Kenny arrived on the sixth floor – though the youth himself still stayed away. Meetings called to launch the union. Meetings about meetings to launch the union. A meeting to choose the chief shop steward – one candidate, Kenneth Glover. I heard John once go up to Brian and suggest that if he was to stand against Kenny, he would surely win. Brian shook his head, didn't want to know. And it made sense, I suppose. It was the fact of the union he deplored. It was that which he was sure would bring Hughes & Hughes to the ground, whoever was running it. And I suppose, in view of subsequent events, he wasn't wrong.

Another time I heard Lawrence speak to Brian privately. He assured him that it wasn't him, Lawrence, who had supplied that last crucial name to the petition. Brian grunted as usual. Seemed about to turn away. Then relented, told the boy he had never thought it was him.

What else happened in those days before New Year's Eve? Perhaps as in the Sherlock Holmes story, it was more remarkable for what didn't happen. For instance, as far as I am aware, Brian never challenged Kenny for his treachery in sending the Dorothy letter to the police. It was as if even something as despicable as this had ceased to have weight or significance in the light of what had happened after. I hated those days. Brian was the main source of the unease that gripped us – but the miasma spread all through the building. Tension everywhere. The great step had been taken – and most of the time, people, even those people who had signed the petition, were wishing rather hard that it hadn't. The future gaped before us now, so uncertain, dangerous, different . . . And yet oddly, behind the dread, I also sensed a kind of nervy exhilaration. A sort of wonder at what had been done. And a pride that Hughes & Hughes too – even us! – was now like the rest of the country: on the move, breaking new ground, swinging head high into the 1960s.

But then the dread would come rolling back in like fog. Altogether there was just too much that felt serious and ominously consequential about those days. It wasn't like Hughes & Hughes at all.

Gradually, I remember, the atmosphere did seem to lighten somewhat, at least in the warehouse. Not because Brian's demeanour improved – it stayed pretty foul. But the boys – and I too – little by little pulled away from the burden of having to imitate it. We were young, even I was young, and could not stay gloomy for ever. I heard little bursts of laughter coming from where the boys were finishing up their inventory. It was quickly stifled out of respect for Brian. And then it would start up again, like a brush fire, so hard to extinguish. I caught them laughing like this one morning. They stopped, seeing my gaze upon them. But something – perhaps the beginning of a smile on my lips – persuaded Lawrence to let me in on the joke. They were remembering the mock-election at their school which had run alongside the genuine one which had taken place last October. A boy called Pitt had stood in the Conservative interest. His posters had borne the simple slogan: 'PITT IS IT!' Of course, it had been the work of a lunch-hour for some imp to go around writing in 'SH' before the last word in the slogan. This was what the boys were laughing at.

I chuckled too. Actually I thought the joke rather low-calibre, but I wanted so much to be part of the fun. And indeed from this small beginning quite a little friendship flowered between the boys and me. Their curiosity having been aroused over the days they had witnessed my silence, they asked me many questions now, of course, but did not attempt to probe where I would not wish them to go. Did not, in other words, ask me why I was barmy. They were most interested to find I had attended university, for both of them were at the stage where they would have to decide whether or not to apply. I dredged up a few anecdotes from my college days, made them sound significantly more frolicsome and enjoyable than they had ever been in real life. The boys liked hearing about them. They wanted to hear more. They asked me out to the pub at lunch-time that day. I went. We had a few beers. I told a few more jolly exaggerations about college. We were chums. And I – I really was no longer the Ghost.

Indeed, if anyone, it was Brian who had donned that mantle. Aloof, gaunt, silent, white-faced, it was him, the spirit of anger and hurt pride, who haunted the sixth floor now. And whereas we youngsters were reverting to our pre-Christmas equanimity – and in my case radically improving on it – the predators that were tearing at him, the disappointment, the hatred, were increasing in fury all the time.

And why not? Downstairs Kenny was busy all day and every day gusting life into the fledgling union, pointing the way to all our futures. And everywhere – except on the sixth floor, of course – Brian was spoken of almost without respect. 'Poor old Bri.' Bit past it. A back-number. Useless. Useless like Mr Hughes.

10

I come now to the most embarrassing confession the narrator of a story can make: I don't know exactly how it ended. For I did not see it. While emotions and enmities were screwing themselves to so dangerous a pitch on the sixth floor, I, on that afternoon, New Year's Eve, was on street level, across the way in the Lady of Kent, listening to the boys explain some scheme they'd run across and that they intended to take up which involved a free passage to New Zealand in return for subsequent help testing milk production among that little country's far-flung cattle herds.

I had no doubt that such a scheme existed. There were still several such in operation then, hangovers from the immediate post-war period, when distant governments, particularly those of the 'older dominions' as I think they were still called, spent significant portions of their budgets to bring in that most prized of immigrants: the white, native Englishman. We were still prized then – just. It was a reassuring undercurrent in all our lives, I think. However stupid, ugly, or generally handicapped, nevertheless we were English, and male, and as such welcome at any Customs and Immigration barrier in the world. We were the prototype still, the blueprint from which all other races and conditions diverged. Now it's completely changed, of course, our status has shrunk utterly. And for all those years of dominance, we are paying heavily. Our historic racism is rightfully condemned. The rest of the world's racism towards us is seen as meritorious, a blow for freedom, we had it coming. Which, after all, we did.

Anyway the boys analysed their hopes and plans exhaustively that lunch-time. So much so that towards the end I thought I saw reality come creeping in, and with it the sad recognition that, like I suspected all their other pipe-dreams, it would never actually come to pass. Tactfully I glanced towards the clock, kindly I suggested it was time to make our way back to Hughes & Hughes to take up our afternoon's labours. And all this while we had been away, according to subsequent reports, guesses, statements, the final argument was brewing on the sixth floor. Kenny had gone up there, would claim his few supporters, to talk in the warehouse about the union. According to those who despised Kenny – and there were many more of those, even though they had signed his petition – the youth had climbed to the top floor, knowing full well that Brian was alone (we were boozing, and Frank had been given a half-day off to visit his mother who had been taken poorly in her nursing-home). Kenny had gone there, said these antis, specifically to tease Brian, to sneer at him for his failure over the petition, revile him. Get his goat. And for evidence of this, it was pointed out that none of the huge amounts of bumph that Kenny had become in the habit of carrying around with him when he was strutting about on union business was found on the sixth floor after the incident.

The incident. What do we know? What did I know, who was trailing at least a floor behind the boys as we made our

176

way upstairs at our separate speeds? Lawrence, who ran everywhere, was first at the sixth-floor doorway. He saw the pair struggling near the loading bay. How had they got over there? Had one lured the other? I never believed what was later reported. It was a cold day, really cold. Nobody would linger in front of that gap, open to the freezing wind, in order to 'just have a chat' (words taken from the inquest).

One got the other over there. For a reason. We'll never know who.

John came into the warehouse next. Lawrence was still standing in the doorway, frozen to the spot. John took the spectacle in quickly, then – a more stolid, practical soul – tried to do something about it. He shouted.

'Watch out!'

That's what I heard, from where I was still on the fifth-floor landing. Not the words, but the note in John's voice, that *fear*, made me first pause, then triple my efforts to get upstairs. I arrived panting in the doorway. What greeted *my* eyes was – nothing. The two boys – Lawrence beside me, John a little way up the gangway – standing stock-still. Beyond them – as I say, nothing. The loading bay gaped emptily on to the sky. But I didn't note it at first as of any importance. The loading bay was usually just like that. Empty. Its square white vacancy only broken by the regular cluster of ropes at the sides, hanging both in and out of the warehouse.

I thought I heard, distantly, a woman scream. And then not John, but Lawrence came alive. He raced up the gangway, past his still-immobilised friend. He got to the loading bay, fell to his knees. Perilously hung out over the abyss.

John now was walking slowly, mechanically up the gangway towards the bay, towards Lawrence. And I came after him.

177

'Hurry!' Lawrence called to us, not looking back. 'One of them's still hanging on.'

All those years ago . . .

1

I heard the worst news first. Poor Lawrence had been killed back in 1970.

'He was twenty-two,' John Brett nodded. '*Bloody shame.*'

We had ordered some food at the health-club bar and had taken it to a table over at the far side of the room, hard by the clinging, spreading glossy vegetation that covered that wall. Like me, John had taken a sparkling mineral water with his sandwiches, but after we'd sat down he'd gazed at the inoffensive drink with dissatisfaction, then had gone back to the bar. He'd returned with two bottles of Rolling Rock. He made a show of offering one to me but I declined, to his evident relief. He'd poured himself a foaming glass; we began to catch up. In a few moments, I was wishing almost that we hadn't.

At university – John explained – Lawrence had joined the mountaineering club. He had turned out to have an aptitude for the sport. In his second year he had been invited to join an Alpine expedition. Did well on it, was asked to come back the following year. In preparation he had gone for a weekend with some other students to the Welsh mountains. There on a simple climb, in no way particularly difficult, he had somehow managed to

181

get himself entangled with his ropes. One of them had tightened around his neck. He had struggled to get free. It made it worse. The others were too far away to reach him in time. When they got to him, he was dead. He had accidentally hanged himself.

I remembered the boy Lawrence. He was as clear to me suddenly as – well, this podgy version of his old friend who now sat before me munching cheese and ham between slices of sesame seed bread. His smile, his lightness, the way he ran everywhere. His socialism. The day Kenny shot him.

Twenty-two.

'Jesus,' I sighed, and John nodded gloomily.

At the time it happened, apparently, the boys had not been close any more. Not that there'd been an estrangement, it was just the way of things when you are young. Their paths had separated after school. John had gone on to study medicine at St Bartholomew's Hospital.

'You're a doctor?'

'Actually no. Couldn't get along with medicine, it turned out. Don't think I ever was much keen on it. Mainly I applied to the school to impress my then girl-friend.'

'Denise.'

He looked at me in surprise. 'You knew her?' And then he remembered. The sacks. And Christmas Eve. He chuckled. 'Ah, yes. Of course you do. Yes,' he nodded, finishing the first Rolling Rock. He poured himself the second. 'Denise Colby. My lord.'

He shook his head, smiling. We were both silent then, both reviewing, I guessed, our memories of the bold, smiling, green-eyed girl who, the second and last time I ever saw her, was clad in that wonderful flame-red duffel coat.

Then, disappointingly, John added, 'Great shag!', and emitted a dirty chuckle.

'She wanted to be a doctor,' I said quickly to stop further elaborations of this nature.

'That's right. I was a year ahead of her in school, didn't know what *I* wanted to do. Then I thought of medical school. At least Denise would be pleased. Stupid thing was –' He shook his head again. 'We broke up during summer term that year. And then I buggered up at Bart's.'

'And Denise? Did she become a doctor?'

He sipped his beer thoughtfully. 'I don't think she did actually. Actually, I think I heard she went into marketing.'

I felt we had re-buried poor Lawrence far too quickly. I wanted to say more about him, some memory, something that would bring him before us for a few more moments as sharply as I had seen young Denise just now. But the curious thing was, though the first time John had mentioned him this afternoon I had seen Lawrence quite clearly, now in my mind's eye his features had become all indistinct. I couldn't hear his voice either. Couldn't remember a thing he'd ever said to me or to anyone else in my hearing. It was as if knowing him now to be dead, my recollection of him too was fast becoming ghostly, buried, unreachable.

I said to John then: 'I'm surprised you were able to recognise me.'

'Pretty good memory for faces,' he nodded complacently.

'But after thirty years? More than?'

'Well, you made quite an impression on us back then.'

'I did?'

'Mm. You were always hanging about back there in the dark. We never knew when we would stumble over you. You were like ... I don't know ...

183

like *ectoplasm*.' He guffawed. 'Guess what we used to call you.'

'The Ghost.' And when he nodded, surprised: 'Brian always called me that. I must have been a hell of a nuisance. It was kind of you not to trouble me.'

'Brian told us not to. He said what you needed was peace and quiet. So we let you alone.'

The name had been spoken twice, the ice was broken. Gingerly at first, and then as if with a long-suppressed hunger, we made our way back to the last appalling day of Brian's long brave reign at Hughes & Hughes.

'Honestly now,' John said, 'what do you think happened that afternoon?'

He was finishing his second beer. He licked his lips. I had an idea he would rather like to switch to something stronger.

I shrugged. 'Kenny said –'

'But of course he would say.'

'– that he'd been talking to Brian and Brian wandered over to the bay –'

'And they stood there talking some more casually –'

'And then Brian slipped –'

'Is it likely? The way he was?'

'I've seen him slip,' I reminded him. 'So have you . . . And then Kenny reached out to save him. And they both went out –'

'And only Kenny hung on.'

A woman's scream. The ropes jerking and dancing. 'One of them's still hanging on.' Wrong one.

'Now I'll tell you what I think happened.' John frowned importantly. I couldn't help noticing that his suit, though I believed of good quality initially, was rather frayed in places. And I suddenly wondered what he was doing hanging around a health club in the middle of the

184

afternoon. Had he nowhere else to go? He had told me what he was doing professionally while we were still at the bar. I couldn't really make head or tail of it. Computers were in there somewhere, inevitably. And a possible medical or pharmaceutical element, I believe. When you sliced it thin enough though, I think a salesman was what he actually was. The closer I looked – the suit, the rather dingy shirt, and the red eyes and veiny nose – the less successful a salesman he appeared to be.

(On the other hand the membership dues at this club were over a thousand a year. On the *other* hand, the bar and restaurant were open to the general public . . .)

'I think it was murder.'

'You think Kenny –?' I started sceptically.

'Yes. Absolutely.' John licked his lips avidly. 'I'll always remember the last thing I ever heard Kenny say to Brian. "I'll fix you." That's what he said. And that's what he did on New Year's Eve.'

'But we all thought that was about reporting Brian to the police on account of Dorothy.'

'It wasn't. It was about murder. I'm sure of it.' John got to his feet then. 'Another one?'

'My round.'

I fumbled for my wallet, but he had already gone.

2

The lunch-time crowd was thinning out. I glanced at my watch. Two-fifteen. The pretty woman I had been admiring before John showed up had gone. There was no one else worth looking at. The gym was settling into its afternoon lull. When I listened for them, I could no longer hear the thud of the treadmills or the whirr and creak of the exer-cycles.

I looked over at John standing at the bar – and then immediately wished I hadn't. He was downing a shot of whisky very fast. I looked away. I hated to feel I had caught him at it. When it was none of my business.

'Have you thought about what I said?'

He settled himself back opposite me. He'd brought with him an untouched double whisky in a tumbler glass, and another bottle of spring water for me. I wished now I had asked for a glass of wine. I didn't want the poor fellow to have to drink alone.

However that wasn't on his mind just now. He was staring intently at me across the glass table.

'I have,' I said.

'What did you think?'

'A bit far-fetched actually.'

'You think Kenny wasn't capable of murder?'

'. . . Perhaps. But I mean – revenge?'

'Not just. *Think* about it. The union wasn't yet launched. Kenny could still have been worrying about what Brian might do. He could even have thought Brian would stand against him in the election.'

I continued to shake my head doubtfully.

'So you believe –?'

'Yes. I think Kenny lured Brian over to the loading bay. Distracted him in some way. Then just pushed him out.'

'But how did Kenny go out too?'

'Just as he was falling –' John's hand rose above the glass table and then pointed downwards. 'Brian grabbed hold of Kenny.'

'To steady himself?'

'To make sure he didn't get away with what he'd done. But,' John mourned angrily, 'he did.'

His hand fell back upon the glass. It was certainly a vivid picture he had painted. I could see Brian dropping away, at the last moment snatching at his killer.

'It sounds as if you were actually there yourself, and had seen it all.'

'I almost feel I was. I just know that's what happened. I thought of going to the police –'

'No proof.'

'Exactly . . . Then I wanted to tell the inquest. Wanted people to know that the poor guy didn't just die in a stupid accident, like that bastard Kenny said. Do you think I should have told 'em?'

I shook my head doubtfully.

'They didn't give us much of a chance to say anything,' I reminded him. 'Just –'

'"What did you see?"' John nodded. 'That's all they wanted to know. No opinions asked for.'

'I didn't see a thing so I wasn't much use.'

'Nor did I hardly. Lawrence saw most. The two of them . . . fighting.'

'Or Kenny trying to keep Brian from falling. Which is what he said in court.'

John grunted. Swallowed more whisky.

'Well, what do you think?' he demanded then, rather brusquely. 'Am I right?'

'Well, it's certainly a theory.'

'It's the truth. Kenny killed Brian for revenge. And to keep him away from the union. And the proof is –' he went on, with a logic I couldn't quite follow, 'look what happened to poor fucking Hughes & Hughes afterwards. Closed within the year, didn't it?'

'Two years. I heard it closed nearly two years later. Of course I'd gone long before then.'

3

The bar was closing and I went over and got a triple whisky for him and a half-bottle of wine for myself. We eased through the rest of that afternoon at our table, being most of the time the restaurant's only occupants. Our conversation drifted this way and that, principally alternating between catching up on our personal lives and reminiscing about those distant events at Hughes & Hughes. I found that, as might happen between any two middle-aged men, our lives had had some points of resemblance, many more that were not. We had both suffered a divorce, for instance, though his had been rancorous and expensive, I gathered, where thankfully mine had not. There were children involved in his, and again I had escaped that. He didn't see his children much; they were living with their mother in the South of France.

'She's French then?'

'No, she just went off to France.'

It seemed that his own circumstances now were not as dire as I had been starting to fear. He was, as I'd guessed, without employment at present, but only because he had recently sold the small business he had owned to a larger rival – for a very nice price, he assured me – and as a condition of this sale he was forbidden to practise his particular professional speciality within London for a period of two years from the sale date. Just now therefore he was spending his time wondering whether to wait out the two years, or to start up in some different business entirely. Which was why he would have an afternoon free such as this to sit around in an empty restaurant with somebody he hadn't seen for over thirty years.

This cheered me quite a lot. Now I could tell myself that the fraying suit and shirt and the grease-spotted tie were just a form of off-duty casual wear. And the drinking – well, poor fellow, the divorce. And he had time on his hands. It was a temporary condition only.

I knew it was kinder to believe this, and certainly more convenient for me. No need really to trouble myself about his circumstances. And actually his drinking grew less fierce as the afternoon wore on. Of course the closure of the bar limited what he could do in that direction, but even when – following some strange timing of his own – the manager opened it up again at about four o'clock, John didn't leap up and charge for the counter, as I might have expected him to do. He only glanced over as the iron grille slid up, and then went back to what he was saying, still continuing to nurse the melted remains of ice in his tumbler, which must have made a very weak alcoholic solution by now.

We were talking about Hughes & Hughes again. Not so much now though about the fatal New Year's Eve. In fact we had both agreed earlier that it was wrong to let that one day, that few minutes of one day, overshadow all the rest. In fact, John said, he hardly ever thought about the tragedy. It was only seeing me that had prompted him to speak of it first today. In fact, it was a negligible detail almost in his memory. And yet over the decades since

190

he'd left it, he'd thought of Hughes & Hughes itself many times.

'I used to bore my friends rigid,' he mused, shifting his large body to a more comfortable position, 'talking about the place. There was something about it, you see – it was as though, if I could understand it, a lot of other things would become clear. It was a sort of symbol –'

'Symbol of what?'

'Not sure. It seemed to change . . . In the 1970s I used to describe it to people as an early instance of what can happen if the unions are allowed to run amok. As they were doing in the 1970s –'

He glanced at me as if to check whether I agreed with that interpretation. I had no reason to argue with it, but kept my expression neutral.

'And I'd talk about Kenny as a sort of a mad dog of union power, Red Robbo –'

'Red Kenny?'

'That's right. The unacceptable face of socialism . . . But then in the Eighties, I started to think: no, that's bullshit. Hughes & Hughes wasn't killed by any union. It was killed because . . . because it had to be! Because it was useless –'

'It was out of date certainly. And terribly inefficient. The stock control, for instance –'

'Exactly – inefficient! Couldn't compete at all. Certainly couldn't compete against the bloody foreigners. Because it was *rubbish*. So perhaps what we saw there was the first application of Thatcherism. Before Thatcher! The original lame duck goes down in flames as it hits real life. In which case . . .' John's expression became puzzled. 'Kenny becomes a sort of benign destroyer, killing all the noxious, evil germs –'

'You mean Brian?'

191

'Oh no!' replied John, shocked.

I leaned forward, suddenly interested in what he was saying. I saw that for a moment he had become tempted to think in unusual, unsettling directions. But then he shook his head firmly.

'No, not at all. I was thinking of – well, the whole useless, failing baggage. Especially Mr Hughes – Christ, do you remember? He couldn't even add up!'

'So Kenny's a White Knight and Hughes & Hughes is a lame duck –?'

'Lame dragon, I suppose, if Kenny's a knight.'

'Is that still how you think of it?'

'How I think of it now . . .' He shrugged. 'I don't know what to think now. I don't know what anything is any more.' (I sympathised with his confusion. I didn't know either. This was '96, we were still living within the long baffling coda to the Thatcher years.) 'Even if I could make Hughes & Hughes a symbol of it, I wouldn't know what it was symbolising . . . I mean everything's changed, that's clear. But what the hell has it changed *into*?'

I couldn't help him.

'It was all so long ago,' he sighed, and I nodded, agreeing. It was.

We were silent for a time, and then he said:

'Funny old place, wasn't it?' He hesitated. 'And yet, it's the strangest thing . . .'

He glanced at me suspiciously, as if fearing I was about to laugh at him. Of course, with no idea what he planned to say, I could do nothing, except wait patiently.

'Yes, it's very odd,' he nodded, 'but ever since, whenever I hear someone talk about heaven – or paradise, you know – well, I mean,' he added hastily, as if wishing to repel any ideas of who he'd been keeping company with over the years, 'on the radio – in the car – religious programmes

192

– or whatever . . . but whenever I hear that – *paradise*, you know – I suddenly get an image of the warehouse at Hughes & Hughes.'

He looked at me again, not suspiciously this time, but almost like a child, as if I could explain something that had been bothering him for decades. As it must have been.

'It's not all that strange,' I said.

'You sure? I just get this warm feeling, as if I'd come home at last.'

'I know what you mean. Christmas Eve, Brian holding forth –'

'Frank cracking walnuts with his fingers.'

'That's right. Lawrence making us all laugh.'

'Lots to eat and drink.'

'And the stuff on the radio. Petula Clark. Freddie and the Dreamers . . .'

'P.J. Proby. Twinkle . . .'

'The Helmut Zacharias Orchestra.'

'What the hell was that?'

I hummed a few bars from 'Tokyo Melody'.

'Oh Christ, *that* . . . Elvis!' he cried out in triumph. '"Blue Christmas"!'

We sang the opening verse together. John was smiling, happiest I'd seen him all afternoon.

'Rotten song really,' he said when we'd finished. 'But God I so often wish I was back up there on the sixth floor, hearing it on the radio . . . And yet it was such a *dump*, wasn't it? Heaven! – Christ, how sad.'

4

He did take on another whisky then, and I think, though can't quite remember, that there was another after that. When at last I told him I had to go, and we got up from the table, he was quite unsteady on his feet. It turned out he had made his way to the health club this afternoon by some other means than in a car. Which, considering his current instability, was certainly a good thing. I offered to drive him home, but that turned out to be towards Putney Common, and as he'd already ascertained that I lived and worked on the Fulham side of the bridge he turned fiercely punctilious and refused to take me out of my way. I persuaded him instead to let me call a minicab for him, and they told me they'd be over in ten minutes.

We waited in the lobby in almost perfect silence, both, I suppose, seeming as if we were still lost in thoughts of the old days. In truth I had begun to consider what I had to do when I got back to my shop. Some new catalogues had arrived this morning, and at first glance there seemed to be certain interesting items that would fit very well into my stock. I would have to go over the lists carefully. Some of the prices I'd glanced at before coming out this morning had seemed far too high, and some weeks earlier I had taken a vow to control this item of expenditure much more carefully in future. The second-hand book business is hardly recession-proof, yet it tends to suffer less than others in the kind of drifting, under-performing economy the country had endured for much of the 1990s (just as it tends to profit less than others in times of boom). All the same I wanted to maintain a downward pressure on my outgoings and above all, to put the danger succinctly, to be careful not to fall in love with some damn book or books and pay far more for them than I could ever get back from my customers.

(Although even that last predicament was never certain. It is an axiom of the business that every book sells at its price in the end, as long as it's displayed. Which is why your average second-hand bookshop is crammed to the rafters with volumes, the whole stock on view at once.)

John's cab arrived at last. I went with him out into the car park. We shook hands. There was an awkward moment where it would have been appropriate for one of us to suggest another meeting. But neither of us did. No reason to really. When it came down to it, our entire acquaintance before this afternoon consisted of a couple of Christmases and the few weeks preceding them back when he was in his teens and I, barely, in my twenties.

Besides, on my side, I suspected that further and closer acquaintance would not make us better friends. I thought I would end up disliking him, in fact. That 'Great shag!' comment about Denise had raised up an early barrier between us. (It consorted so ill with my memories of the boy John's sweetly shy and hesitant demeanour as he had led his girl to their tryst among the sacks so long ago.) And there was the drinking too and the general air of disorder he now carried around with him, which I found repellent. I sound like a prude saying this – what I mean is that I concluded there in the car park that, in his middle age, life's stern blows had turned John into a bit of a wild man. I had gone through all that upheaval and confusion when I was still young, and ever since had tried to avoid others who were in a similar fix, for I feared it might be catching, and I couldn't afford a repeat dose.

'Well . . . probably see you around here some time,' John said at last, and I agreed that it was likely.

He had turned from me, had started towards the cab, when he came to a halt. I wondered if he needed my help to get him loaded inside the cab, and was about to ask him just this, when he turned back to me. There was a half-smile on his face. It was a knowing sort of smile, as if he had a naughty secret and wanted to share it.

He watched me for a moment, then he nodded.

'It was you, wasn't it?'

'It was me?'

'You were the last one to sign Kenny's petition. Weren't you? You gave him that final name he needed. To get the union started.'

We stared at each other. Behind him, the cab driver bipped impatiently on his horn.

'It was you,' he repeated. 'Am I right?'

'Oh, yes,' I said. 'It was me.'

He nodded, satisfied.

'I worked it out with Lawrence afterwards. Really, it couldn't have been anyone else, could it?'

5

I went down to Cutt Street on my next half-day off – rather
I went to where Cutt Street had been. It wasn't there any
more, of course. I hadn't expected it to be. The last time I
had set foot in the neighbourhood was on a day in the early
1970s, '71, '72, when, with some time to waste before
catching a train, I had thought it might be interesting to
have lunch in the old Lady of Kent. Not possible, as it
turned out. The pub (whose foundations were those of the
first hostelry on the site, dating from 1460 it was said) was
no more. Like every other structure around, it had been
reduced to a pile of half-cleared builders' rubble.

I did wonder what the patch might have become since
then as I drove through all the southern riverine villages
– Wandsworth and Battersea and Nine Elms, and past
the bridges: Vauxhall, Lambeth, Westminster. Wondered
whether it had been buried under something properly
emblematic of our day and age. Perhaps Cutt Street
was a shopping mall now, or a drive-thru Burger King,
or was lined with 'exciting riverside developments' and
'affordable homes for the 21st century'. The latter was
my best guess.

I went past Waterloo Station where my train deposited
me every weekday morning when I was twenty-one,

197

twenty-two. After that a bus along Stamford Street, and on past Blackfriars and Southwark Bridges. Even after the tragedy, I kept showing up here, getting out of the train, switching to the bus, like an automaton. I stayed at Hughes & Hughes for three months after Brian's death. I actually had serious thoughts of making a real career there. And why should I not? It's an ill wind, etc. Post-tragedy, I was rising in the firm.

It should have been Frank, of course. I had said this to John in the restaurant when we were going over what had happened at Hughes & Hughes after he'd left. He agreed with me. He was astonished that Frank had been passed over.

'How could they? And him the brother!'

'Cousin,' I reminded. 'But you're right. It was outrageous.'

'So –' John eyed me incredulously. 'You were the new Brian?'

'In a manner of speaking. Though it was made clear to me it was just a temporary appointment. While things got sorted out.'

But I hadn't believed it. Rather I believed that if I really showed what I could do, they'd have to give me the job permanently. Just like in a story-book. And so the truth is, in those weeks after Brian's death, when I might have been supposed to be giving all my thoughts – or at least more than just a fraction of them – towards mourning our hero's tragic end, I was giving everything I had in order to show how neatly and usefully I could slip into his shoes.

'How did Frank take it? Being passed over? I mean he'd been there –'

'Twenty-five years. Oh, he was fine ... Well, no,' I shrugged. 'He was very hurt, of course he was. I could see it. I should have turned the job down. But –'

But I didn't. I was so intoxicated with this promotion. So pleased to be *somebody* in the building after years of being not even a nobody. Just ectoplasm. The Ghost. And I'm sure it was good for me. To have that responsibility, even that small authority. It was therapy you couldn't buy, you might say. And the proof is: when the job was taken away from me – after I had worked so fucking hard at it, after I had *deserved* to keep it – I didn't crack up, didn't go to pieces. There was no reverting to the Ghost. Instead, I did the healthy thing. I quit.

'Frank was fine working with me. We were a good team. He accepted me as chief storeman.'

'But Kenny was the last straw?'

I couldn't believe it. Mr Hughes had come up to the sixth floor that Monday morning. Kenny was smirking and lurking behind him. Frank and I had started collecting for the first delivery, him calling as ever from the invoices, me working in the shelves just as Brian always had. Of course we were nowhere near as fast as when *he* was doing it. But we did all right. We got the job done and always in time.

'Thank you for holding the fort so admirably,' Mr Hughes told me. He was wearing his characteristic brave, defeated smile that I usually found rather endearing, but which today, almost immediately, would prompt in me the desire to knock it off his face. 'Kenny will be taking over now.'

'Taking over?'

'That's right. If you wouldn't mind going back to the dusting.'

Frank left that same day. I think he went without a word to his cousin. He gave me a telephone number. I lost it very soon after, never saw or heard from him again. I suppose I should have left immediately too, but I was dazed somehow by the cascade of events and I hung around for a few days more. Kenny, expressing relief that

'that idiot' had departed from 'his' warehouse, strutted around self-importantly, informing me about the way he planned to run things now. I didn't listen to him much, though I did notice when he graciously 'promoted' me to Frank's old job. I stood calling the invoices for a few mornings and watched him leaping among the tiers. He was pretty good at the jumps, about a half as good as Brian had been, but when he got to where he had to fill the paper bags, he rather lost interest, stuffing them with haphazard amounts of our stock before chucking them on to the table. He was all style in fact, and the content – certainly the contents – could go hang. We were starting to get some very aggrieved phone calls from our clientele. Kenny's telephone manner was not emollient. Several old customers became ex-customers on the spot.

'But why on earth did Hughes give Kenny the job?' John had asked me.

'To buy him off. Because he was scared of the union.'

That's what I firmly believed at the time. Everyone knew that Mr Hughes was being confronted with ever-escalating union demands. It must have appeared to him a shrewd, a Machiavellian move to placate the apparent leader of the insurgency by giving him Brian's old job, shoving me aside in the process. If so, he was sorely mistaken. Kenny's tenure as a labour leader was very brief. I had heard rumbles about 'the way he was carrying on' even before that New Year's Eve. A strong candidate from the fourth floor (Personnel) appeared to run against him in the ballot for union officers. Kenny withdrew before the vote, unwilling to face the shame of a heavy defeat. He affected not to care, and perhaps he didn't. He had got his hands on the job that I think he must have always secretly coveted in the days of Brian's glory. And as the song goes, now the working class could kiss his arse. In fact, in the brief period when Kenny and I were in sole tenure of the warehouse I heard him once refer to his erstwhile union connections as a 'bunch of f——n' trouble-makers'.

But after it was over, I began to think that this interpretation of my downfall and of Kenny's promotion was far-fetched. We all like to think that our setbacks can only be the result of tortuous and illegitimate manoeuvring. In fact, I concluded in the end that the explanation was probably much more simple. That when I had been given Brian's old job, it was – as, in fairness, I must say it had been told me at the time – a temporary measure only. That my occupancy of the post was always uncertain, and in a way incredible, given my past history in the company, and a few weeks of hard slogging on my part were not going to change that. That when I was, finally, got rid of, it was a recognition that I had no future at Hughes & Hughes. No business really being there, now I was no longer the Ghost.

I agreed. A few days of watching the obscenity of Kenny trying to ape his great predecessor's style and competence, and then one morning I went down to the ground floor and told Mr Hughes that I wanted to leave. He made no fuss about me having to give my notice and said I could go right away if I wanted. As I was leaving, he came to the door and shook my hand and thanked me for everything I had done. It was extraordinary – I wanted to cry, and I hadn't even done that as we'd stood out in the street, New Year's Eve, beside Brian's body.

The last person I saw at Hughes & Hughes was Hoover, who was coming into the building just as I was going out. I told her she was looking cheerful, and she tossed back her yellow mane.

'I ought to be,' she beamed. 'My daughter came home last night. Oooh, I gave her such a hiding!'

6

My anticipation of finding that the old Cutt Street area had been turned into some ironic, post-modern statement was not to be fulfilled. Where the street had been, and Hughes & Hughes with it, was now a riverside housing estate. And no gigantesque 'project' this either. A few short roads lined with two- and three-storey apartment buildings. I think they must have been put up about twenty years ago, and the yellow and red brick of their exteriors was ageing nicely. I wasn't quite certain if these were council dwellings. I saw a Range Rover in one of the driveways, but that might not have meant anything. There was an absence of estate agent boards, which may have been more significant.

It was a wholly unexceptionable little area. Modest, worthy, undramatic. I wouldn't have minded living there. It seemed suddenly absurd, on this bright spring day, to feel nostalgic in any way for the old black Dickensian horrors that used to stand here. And the greasy cobblestones that we slipped and slid on. As we had done that awful day, running from the building to join the shocked crowd that had gathered outside. John had led the way, pushing towards the centre. Inside the ring lay Brian. Somebody had already laid a raincoat over him to cover his head and chest and shoulders. Blood leaked from under it. It was a woman's raincoat, I remembered, a purplish colour. I looked up. High above me was the gaping bay and out of it, Kenny was peering down at us. It might have been the murderer looking at his foul deed. In fact, I believed it was more probably the intended victim staring down upon his would-be assassin.

This was my theory. The one I had chosen not to share with John that afternoon. I had been convinced of it, from almost the moment we had pulled Kenny up, kicking, bellowing in fear, back into the warehouse. For I remembered how Brian had been those days after Christmas. Brooding all the time. I'd never seen him like that before. It was frightening. And I knew the reason for it. Kenny had got his names and the union was a cert now. And Brian was sure that, between them, Kenny and the union were going to finish off Hughes & Hughes –

So he decided to finish off Kenny.

This I saw in my mind's eye that day, and for some long time afterwards: that he had got Kenny over to the window. Lured him over. So he could throw him out. It was in character after all; he'd done that at least once before. True, on that occasion he had made sure Kenny was holding on to a rope.

But not this time. This time it was going to be for keeps. For the sake of Hughes & Hughes . . . Only Kenny was too quick for him. After all – what was he? Nineteen? And Brian? Thirty-two? Thirty-three? He'd lost his edge. He'd had a bad fall not long before. He wasn't himself . . . There was a struggle. They both went out. But Kenny hung on –

And Brian didn't.

His last amazing arc through the air had ended with him stretched out down there, looking like a poor big broken doll, on the cobbles far below.

He had laid down his life. Trying to save his friends. His work-mates. Mr Hughes. A sacrifice. My hero.

At least that's how I saw it for a time. Now, on the rare occasions when I look back on those days, that day, I'm not so sure. My convictions have drifted, turned into smoke. Now I'm not certain if it really wasn't just an accident as Kenny had claimed. Or some mixture of accident and mischief. Dangerous horseplay, and perhaps somebody gave a last sly foolish push without really considering what it might mean. Which sounded like Kenny. But hardly premeditated.

I went to sit on a bench that was sited on a patch of grass by the river. The view across the water to the north bank was very fine. I knew I ought to be mourning the fact that the river was almost free of traffic – meaning decline, loss of jobs, shattered neighbourhoods, all that – whereas in my memories of thirty years ago it had been thick with trade. Of course, in those days, we couldn't actually see the river because of the warehouses lining it, but always in our hearing were the growl and clank of the engines and the endless tootings of the ships' whistles.

But unarguably this was a fine sight – and anyway much of the trade (if not many of the jobs) that had been here once was no doubt still being carried on, somewhere further down, at the vast mechanised terminals nearer the sea. Leaving this immense and satisfying prospect . . . and it came to me again how silly it was to be so automatically nostalgic about those grimy old days. All gone now, as gone and forgotten as the people. Thank God. Once in the early 1980s I had read a report in the newspaper about a Kenneth Glover under arrest for some dodgy Spanish time-share scheme. The accompanying photo could have been Kenny, an older, bald, moustachioed Kenny. Of course I'd never bothered to try and find out.

7

There were a couple of odd-looking, unmoving figures further along the bank. I got up and went to investigate. Both were cast in metal. Both in the costumes of a century ago. A little girl standing at the river wall. From a bench a metal man was pointing at her. Near them was an explanatory text mounted on a podium. The little girl turned out to be the man's daughter – his angel. The light of his life. The man was a doctor who, at the turn of the century, had done much for the huge numbers of poor people who lived in the area then. The doctor's little girl had died, still a child, of scarlet fever. No doubt caught from the doctor's patients. His light had gone out.

I turned away, and I knew there were tears in my eyes. Prompted by the sad little story of the doctor and his child, but not really for them. Not so much for Brian even. I don't know what for actually. I thought of the immeasurable misery that must have lined the river a hundred years ago. There was the period of that. Then there must have come a period when the tenements and the horrors were partly cleared away. Then – what? – the war. Destruction raining from the skies night after night and the great fires starting. Amazing that so much had been left still standing. Then after the war, more clearing up. And then the period I knew – of the early 1960s. New people in the old buildings. So it went on. Period after period – and what was I longing for now, weeping for, over thirty years after?

Is heaven for the English, I wondered – *or was it once* – just this: some idea of a community, a brotherhood, nominally headed up by an inefficient but well-meaning patriarch, actually run by and kept in line by stern but fair non-commissioned officers? A community dedicated to . . . nothing much. Certainly not efficiency. Or profit. Or getting ahead. Just the being there was enough, the ring around the fire, the warmth, the jokes, the comfort against the cold, the joy of knowing one's exact place in the circle.

John's lost paradise.

Hughes & Hughes.

Well, I took care of that.

Until the other day, I had never told anybody what I had done. That the last signature on Kenny's petition had been mine. I was very frightened that he would expose me – as he would have done, I am sure, if it had occurred to him to do so. But he was in such a state of excitement at being the man of the moment – Kenny the Father of the Union – that for once he hadn't an ounce of time or attention to spare on mere conventional mischief. So a few days of sickening fear passed for me, and then came New Year's Eve and after that it didn't matter. Brian would never know now.

Except, deep down, I was sure he *had* known. He was too intelligent not to have. Too aware of the human material he had been given to work with . . . And I couldn't forget that the moment I had finished reading Mr Hughes' letter announcing his acquiescence to the union, I had looked around at Brian – to find him staring coldly, directly at me. Oh, he *knew*.

Given that he did, I wished afterwards he had asked me why I had done it. Perhaps under that compulsion I could have come up with an answer that made some sort of sense. Without it I certainly couldn't. I could have said I was drunk when I'd done the damn thing. Which was no more than the truth. So drunk that I had hardly any memory of the deed when I woke up the next day, and certainly no sense of the importance of it. All through Christmas I was sublimely unconcerned. And in fact it was only as my train drew in at Waterloo, the morning after Boxing Day, that it really hit me what had happened on Christmas Eve. My pace as I went to join the bus queue was awfully slow that morning.

Drunkenness was the context in which I had signed the petition – I never felt it provided the whole answer as to why I had done it. Sometimes, in the years that followed, as I looked back – fleetingly, furtively as at a squalid little crime – I tried to believe that I had been motivated, however foolishly, by some vague desire to promote the general good. This was especially the case in the 1970s, as industrial strife spread through the country, and there seemed to be a new heroic union battle launched every week. In this light I stepped forward as a modest but sincere pioneer of the struggle, and my small but vital act in providing the last necessary signature was not a breathtaking piece of treachery, but a serious attempt to bring order and fairness and rationality to the chaotic medieval world of Hughes & Hughes.

Mostly though I knew this was rubbish. That whatever had motivated my action was not born out of rationality and right thinking. I remembered often that I had found myself unexpectedly angry with Brian that afternoon. It seemed to centre around the odd little episode of the policeman. Detective-Sergeant Ames. How for a moment I had had a vision of Brian being put under arrest, taken away, dislodged permanently from his sixth-floor fortress. And I remembered too that I had rather enjoyed this vision – and had been quite annoyed when Brian had characteristically side-stepped the danger.

Was it then that, as much as poor vile Kenny, I had wanted to bring Brian down? This was such a painful thought to me – my hero, my lost leader – that it was years before I could bring myself to look at it squarely. And yet I had to concede in the end that it was a possibility. As I was emerging from my ghost-like state, it was quite likely that I would conceive some form of animus against the kindly dictator who had ruled me in my weakness. In any case, it is natural for men to spar, resent domination, seek the throne. Look at the progression of events: I sign the petition, as a result Brian dies, as a result I step – for a time – into his shoes. I become king of the sixth-floor castle. I am a black-hearted assassin.

More time, and a fading taste for melodrama moved me away from this exciting interpretation. I knew I hadn't hated Brian, knew I had loved him really – and resented him probably, a little, but never nearly enough to plot his downfall, let alone his death. And how could I have known that a little thing like a signature – scrawled out, between tipsy giggles on the third-floor landing, under Kenny's gloating eyes – could have led to such a ghastly issue?

Once I think I saw the truth. It lay in another memory from that Christmas Eve. The happiest of memories. We are all sitting around in a circle – Brian, Frank, myself, the two boys, Denise. (The ring of backs against the cold, the joy of knowing one's place, all of that . . .)

And we are full of food and booze, already we are feeling so sloppy-sentimental, so *Christmassy* – and at just that moment the band below starts up with 'Silent Night'.

And I couldn't *stand* it any more. This humble, frowsty paradise. This safe, smug, cosy prison on the sixth floor. The whole mediocre boiling – could not bear it a moment longer. And so, later on, when the evil imp prompted me to do what I wanted to do – yes, I was ready. To smash things. Kick over the traces. Kill the past. To change the present. See what would happen next. Child of my time. Child of the 1960s. Angry child.

So I signed that petition – on the third floor, that Christmas Eve, because the Salvation Army had played 'Silent Night', and we were all so close, and it was all so fucking perfect, and I *couldn't stand it any more*. I signed it, and brought everything down. I stormed heaven and then broke it apart. Mainly to see what would happen next.

Cobbles, greasy in the drizzle. The purple mantle. A pair of jeans-encased legs stuck out at angles from under it. Blood seeping . . . But even so – wouldn't I do it again? Of course I would. Perhaps not now. But then – oh, certainly. Didn't history demand it?

8

It was time to go home. Past time, I suspected. In my ravenous search for some meaning in all that old confusion, I was starting to feel too close to the shade of poor John Brett, as I remembered him at the health club, groping after 'symbols' among his own fuddled memories of Hughes & Hughes. Of course he had found them – as I had found them. It's so easy; they are lying around waiting to be picked up, for almost everything takes on the peculiar patina and resonance of its time to some degree.

And, with passing time, loses it. In the present moment – in this orderly little housing estate – the rude ghosts of long ago, though for a while they could be induced to flicker forth again, had grown faint indeed. Faint and far away as the Ghost himself. Whose distant descendant now retraced his steps to where he'd parked the car.

There was a deep fresh scar upon the driver's door, and then past that along the panel that held the headlight. I looked around. There was no one to see. Mainly to take some of the sting out of this commonplace disaster, I tried to imagine that the spirit of Kenny had been at work here while I'd been mooning about beside the river. It was a Kennyish sort of thing to do, I supposed: stupid, envious, destructive. But the fancy didn't really hold me, and as I was driving towards the main road I passed a knot of boys, early teens, shouting and larking about, almost certainly the culprits. One of them – a little sod in a New York Yankees baseball cap – grinned at me as I went by and pointed to the side of my car as at a job well done.

I crossed Tower Bridge and took the north bank route home. There were hold-ups near Westminster – placards along the way informed me that the head of a country I'd never heard of was paying a state visit and delays were expected, etc. I dropped a 1960s compilation into the deck and waited it out with Ray and Dave:

> 'As long as I gaze on
> Waterloo sunset
> I am in paradise.
> Sha-la-lah . . .'

Ah, yes, and nothing new under the sun. It was nearly six o'clock by the time I reached the end of New King's Road. I hadn't intended going to the shop. Lately I'd been consciously trying to avoid doing that on my half-days off. Arguably, I needed the time away to refresh myself. Also it was a vote of confidence in my staff (of three), showing my belief that the business could be kept up satisfactorily in my absence.

Certainly I didn't doubt that – but even so I turned off into the cul-de-sac opposite the shop where I had parking rights. Some traces of melancholy still clung to me from my visit to the past today, to what had been Cutt Street. I wanted company. And I wanted tangible, visible proof that everything had moved on since back then, and had got better. I wanted to confirm the distance I had come.

For a moment I stood in front of my shop, looking it over, feeling my pride grow as I gazed. Truthfully, I don't know of a more *satisfactory-looking* bookstore of its type in all of London. The windows sparkled – I insisted on that, no second-hand murk and dust for me. The display itself always reflected, I hoped, a judicious balance between Old and Newish, between fairly rare and pretty common. At the moment a fine example of Victorian book-making – *A Book of Favourite Modern Ballads* (1860), opened to the title page and so showing the excellent engraving and colour printing of Birket Foster and Edmund Evans – dominated the centre ground. But I had around it piles of Gollancz Mysteries in their cheerful red and yellow jackets, and behind them a fan-shaped display of Patrick O'Brian titles. I think it all worked. I wanted us to look special, even distinguished, but not repellently so.

The rest of the shop-front also, I believed, carried this quality of unpretentious distinction. I had got the particular shade of paint used on it from a speciality shop in Notting Hill Gate. It was called – this is true – 'Graham Green': a cool, rather astringent hue that just now, in the waning light, was losing itself into black. Yet the name I had chosen for the shop still gleamed forth in its letters of gold. I suppose this name was the only bit of waywardness I had allowed myself in setting up the business. I thought I could not afford more than one. In many ways the shop had represented my last chance in life. For there had been no miraculous ascension into grace after I'd quit being the Ghost. On the contrary that only served to launch me on a career which – starting with being bounced out of college on my second attempt at a degree, then going through one of those dizzying series of half-jobs and wacko ventures that used to make up the standard biogs of paperback writers – had left me by my early thirties living in a squalid little room in somebody else's flat, virtually unemployable, and with a small but steadily growing cocaine habit to maintain.

My parents had both then died within the same eighteen-month span and, equally with my brother, I had divided their estate: the house, some shares, a bit of money. I could have chosen to jam it all up my nose. But by now I was bone-weary of all that. Sick of being such a failure (very sorry that that condition was the last my parents had known of me). The question was: what other choices were there? I thought it over with all the concentration I could then summon up. It came to me at last that among all my various whims and fantasies, I did have a real though hitherto intermittent interest in books, particularly old books, a curiosity that, as I've described, I could trace back to my Auntie May's eccentric gift on that fatal Christmas of '64. I went around and around this notion, and at last resolved to take the plunge. I used a little of my parents' money to keep myself going while I learned the ropes at a shop in Shepherd's Bush. Then I found this business up for sale on the unfashionable end of New King's Road. I used the rest of my inheritance to buy the shop's lease, stock, goodwill, the lot. I put a bed in the back room. It was my home now. If it didn't work out I'd be on the street, literally.

Very carefully, taking all the advice I could get, working twenty hours out of the twenty-four, I gradually turned around what had been up till then a moderately dwindling concern. And, as I say, in setting things up in the beginning, I permitted myself to stray from the straight and narrow only in the matter of the shop's name. Which in fact was not the sort of deviation that was likely to cause any disquiet, or even be noticed. Even my soon to be ex-friends, who came around in the early days to see how I was doing – and whether I could use a gram, great stuff, good price – only thought I hadn't bothered to change the name of the previous ownership. Really, it was just my little peccadillo, quite private. I hadn't, for instance, mentioned the name to John that afternoon we'd met in the health club.

I went inside. My foot striking the mat sent up a tuneful 'ping-pong'. Marie looked up from near the cash-point and smiled reprovingly at me. She knew I had taken those vows about keeping away entirely on my half-days. She knew most things about me. We had been – well, lovers, I suppose, for nearly a year. We were at a stage where both were trying to decide if it was right to take the next step and move in together. It seemed a very solemn move to contemplate. She was in her early forties, I past fifty. At that age one feels there will be no easy wriggling out of such a commitment. It must be for the long term, perhaps for as long as mortality allows. And is this person really the person one wants to see at the end of the day? On this last throw of the dice, couldn't one do better? Well, *couldn't* one? We were both very thoughtful people at this time.

Yet we were good pals too, and that was the best promise for a happy outcome. I grinned back at her, to show yes, I knew I was being a naughty boy, shouldn't be here really, but there you are . . . We had tickets for the Queen Elizabeth Hall tonight. That was a good thought – an anti-Ghost thought – to hold as I made my way through the shop. Peter, the ex-Durham University student – crashed out in his second year, same year as I had at another place a quarter-century before – was with a customer over in the Aeronautical Section. Like most second-hand booksellers, I have my areas of specialisation. Early Aircraft was one. Theatre Criticism. The American Civil War. Pre-Commonwealth Australia. I am trying to develop too a presence in natural history, mainly because I like handling and looking at the volumes so much. But

214

there are so many established collections in those fields that the effort is probably misplaced.

Janet Coombes, ex-Foyles, ex-Zwemmers, who has been with us for ten years, was in the end room entering new stock on the Compaq. We have been computerised for some time now. My accountant sent a man along to tell us what we needed. Someone somewhere had thought it worthwhile to write a software programme just for such businesses as ours, and we soon had it up and running. Only Janet though really knows all its intricacies, and I tell her once in a while that she never needs to worry about me firing her given that, computer-wise, nobody else understands what the hell is going on.

Actually that isn't true. Janet's job – like Peter's, like, I suppose, even Marie's – depends on their continuing usefulness to the business. Nothing else. We all do work hard here. There are no slackers. Nobody lurking among the darkness of the shelves, without a real job to do. No Ghosts with feather dusters. I won't have that. I haven't got so little pride in myself, or respect for my colleagues, that I would allow that. If it ever became necessary, I would be prepared to downsize like – to use the idiom of Bob Paco, a young American who worked for us for a few months in '92 – like gangbusters.

So, yes, I run a tight ship. I am tight, narrow, wary. And successful within my own small compass. In truth, I thought that evening, as I stood breathing in the good brown smell of my shop, I had nothing much to regret as I looked back down the years, all the way to that time on Cutt Street. There had been casualties along the way. I regretted them. But they had been necessary, I supposed.

215

I thought of the making of omelettes, the breaking of eggs
. . . Janet looked up at me then. Waved. I smiled back at her,
turned away to look at the fiction shelves. My stock of first
editions from the 1920s and 1930s was bulking up nicely,
I saw. Another Dornford Yates had just been added.

The phone on Janet's desk rings. She makes a face. She's
awfully busy. I go and pick it up. Press it to my ear.

'Hughes & Hughes?' I say.

May 1997

A NOTE ON THE AUTHOR

Peter Prince is the author of several novels including *Play Things* (winner of the Somerset Maugham Award), *The Good Father* and *Death of the Soap Queen*. His screenplays include the award-winning BBC TV series *Oppenheimer* and the feature film *The Hit*. He lives in London.